CW00549319

Windsor Christmas Tales

Windsor Writers' Group

This book is published by Windsor Writers Group, UK, 2021.

ISBN: 979-8-48040-960-4

ACKNOWLEDGEMENTS

Along with all the contributors to this anthology, the Windsor Writers' Group would also like to thank Ruth Brandt for the Foreword, Bryony Marianne Usher for the illustrations, June Kerr for the cover illustration and Pauline Wells for creating the cover artwork.

FOREWORD

By

Ruth Brandt

This collection of seasonal stories takes the reader along the streets of Windsor, past the Castle, through the Great Park, into shops and homes, and down side alleys. And while Christmas lights twinkle and the chill winter wind blasts us, we meet royal ghosts, and love-matching ghosts, and sentient trees. We experience floods, slip back in time, and return to the very real problems of homelessness on Windsor's streets. We even take a trip on Concorde. Yet, throughout we are reminded of what it is to be human at Christmas, of absent family and friends, of moments of self-reflection, and generosity.

The Windsor Writers' Group Christmas Anthology brings the spookiness, mystery and magic of Christmas to life while celebrating the wonder and majesty of Windsor.

Ruth Brandt
Writer and Creative Writing Tutor
Christmas 2021.

CONTENTS

ILLUSTRATIONS
By

Bryony Marianne Usher

Bryony is an illustrator from Windsor who studied at Arts University Bournemouth. She was the winner of the Lauren Child Poetry Illustration Prize 2018 and was longlisted for the Templar Illustration Awards 2020. Combining the free, textural exploration of painting, drawing and printmaking with the refinement and adaptability of digital design, she explores the ways light, colour and texture can enhance emotion and bring to life the stories we tell.

See more of her work on www.bryonymarianne.com and follow her on Instagram & Facebook – you can find her at @bryonymarianne.illustration.

ABOUT THE AUTHORS

Jonathan Posner
Jonathan has written and published three novels, as well as three stage musicals and a one-act play. When not writing he works in animal health advertising.
Contact: https://jonathanposnerauthor.com

Adrian McBreen
Adrian has been writing short stories for a few years. He is currently working on a longer creative piece, which is filed under 'N' in his documents folder, also known as a novel. He would recommend joining a local writers' group, as a motivation and inspiration to keep writing.
Contact: https://windsorwriters.co.uk

Helena Marie
Helena has had several poems published in anthologies and online. More recently she has turned her pen to short stories, two of which are included here, and is writing her first novel. She has recently begun an MA in Creative Writing, and is excited to see where that leads her.
Contact: https://windsorwriters.co.uk

Wendy Gregory
Wendy Gregory is a Counselling Psychologist and writer. She has been published in several magazines, such as Happiful, Cosmo, Woman and Metro and has self-published a book for young people: "The Little Book Of Retorts – A teenager's Guide To Beating The Bullies," which is available from

www.thelittlebookofretorts.com, Wendy is also a regular guest Psychologist on Talk Radio and Times Radio.
Contact: https://windsorwriters.co.uk

Sue Blitz
For the past 20 years, Sue has lived and worked in Windsor. An advertising copywriter all her working life she has always enjoyed the power of words. Her first children's book was published last year and she has another one in the pipeline.
Contact: https://windsorwriters.co.uk

Amanda Buchan
After reading English and French at University in New Zealand and England, Amanda worked in Arts Administration and Educational Aid, travelling worldwide. She has lived in Windsor for twenty years with her sons and cat. She writes poetry and stories and is writing a memoir about adapting to different cultures.
Contact: https://windsorwriters.co.uk

Rosa Carr
Rosa Carr is the author of the young adult fantasy novel, Air Fay. She grew up in South Africa but has made the UK home. She is a psychology student, formerly a librarian, and now working in publishing.
Contact: https://rosacarr.com

June Kerr
Originally from Scotland, June has lived south of the border for more years than she'd like to count and in the Windsor area for the last 30. Initially writing purely for self-indulgence, June has since had various magazine articles published and has recently finished her memoir, 'Confessions of an alcoholic air hostess,' hoping it will become the next best-selling airport novel?
Contact: https://windsorwriters.co.uk

Robyn Kayes

Robyn is from South Africa and always wanted to travel. She toured the world as a travel agent, then worked for an airline. She moved to the UK with her family and lives in Windsor. Writing short stories is a newfound interest.

Contact: https://windsorwriters.co.uk

Kanthè

My artist name is Kanthé and I have received awards and prizes for my poetry and short stories. I am also a visual artist and currently contributing to an online exhibition. Eleven of my poems and five art pieces have been published - I am currently working on my first novel.

Contact: Twitter: @kanthe2000

Vivien Eden

Vivien has loved living in Windsor since the noughties. The town has provided her with endless stimuli for penning a short story, churning out a Haiku or two or attempting yet another opening chapter of a book. Her latest project is a children's dystopian novel that she *will* finish.

Contact: https://windsorwriters.co.uk

Phil Appleton

Phil Appleton began writing in 1981 and has recently published his memoir Blue Sky Red Carpet. An actor and communications skills coach, he has also been an airline pilot, a VIP Handling Officer, and a legal interpreter. A Windsor resident for 15 years, he has worked with local young adults to improve their interview, presentation, and impact skills.

Contact: www.blueskyredcarpet.com

1

A Windsor Christmas Carol

Jonathan Posner

The small, balding man barrelled down the street from Windsor Castle, leaving Christmas shoppers bobbing about like so much flotsam in his wake.

Glancing up at the illuminated decorations, he muttered to himself, "Complete waste of time and money!" Then he added, "Nothing whatsoever to do with Christmas!"

Making a sharp left turn at the bottom of Peascod Street, he marched into the parcel pick-up room at the back of the Post Office and thumped on the bell. Precisely two seconds later, he thumped on it again.

"Service!" he barked at the empty desk behind the glass screen. "Service!"

Three rings later, the door behind the desk swung open with an almost insolent slowness. A head appeared. "Yes?"

The small man pushed a red-bordered card through the opening in the screen.

"Parcel!"

The head came further round the door, and a Post Office employee in a grey polo shirt was revealed. He ambled up to the counter.

The balding man tapped on the card. "Parcel!" He paused expectantly, but the employee did not pick up the card. "Parcel! Parcel!" he repeated, anger now tinged with an edge of desperation.

The Post Office man took the card and studied it, first one side, then the other, as if to assure himself that he had discovered its every secret.

"A minute," he said, pulling at his earlobe as he studied both sides of the card again. Then he put his hand to the door as if to push it but stopped and studied the card one more time. "One minute," he repeated, and pushed through the door.

Exactly one minute and six staccato rings on the bell later, the Post Office man returned, carrying a brown cardboard package about the size of a shoebox.

"Name?"

"Pierce. Warren Pierce. P-I-E-R-C-E."

"ID?"

Warren pushed his passport through the opening. The Post Office man licked his finger and turned the pages until he came to the information spread, audibly cracking the spine as he forced it open. Then he studied the picture carefully. He looked up at Warren, then back at the picture.

"Address?"

"105 Fountain Gardens, Windsor." Warren paused as the man looked up at him with an eyebrow raised.

"Postcode?"

"Sierra Lima 4, 3 Sierra Uniform."

The man pushed the cardboard box through the gap and wandered back through the door.

Warren grabbed his package and almost ran out of the room. Retracing his steps up William Street, he turned left onto Peascod Street, continuing to head away from the Castle. As he strode along, he snapped at no one in particular, "Total waste of time! No sense of urgency, these people! Nothing better to do! Disgrace! Blasted disgrace!"

A small knot of people was gathered on the pedestrianised street in front of him, obstructing his path. As he started to march round them, he noticed that in the centre of the crowd there was a man with a large video camera and another man holding a big grey furry microphone on a pole. The camera man was filming a girl in a pale cream wool sweater who was facing him, her breath making small vapour clouds in the clear air. The sound man was holding his microphone close to her waist.

Despite his urge to get home as quickly as possible, Warren's curiosity got the better of him, He found himself slowing and stopping, then peering between the shoulders of the crowd to see what was happening.

The girl in the sweater finished talking to the camera, then accepted a take-away cup of coffee from a scruffy-looking girl in an old parka jacket next to her. She took a swig from the cup, gave it back, then took out her phone and started tapping furiously on the screen with her thumbs.

Warren decided that the show was over and was just about to resume his journey, when the girl put the phone back in her pocket and looked around at the crowd. Her gaze briefly met Warren's, then passed on to the person next to him.

Then flicked back to Warren.

As he watched, she nudged the girl in the parka, pointed at him and said something out of the side of her mouth.

The girl then pushed her way up to him. She had little white sticks protruding from her ears, and a faint tinny sound of music could just be heard.

"'Scuse me," she said, "we're getting some opinions on the commercialisation of Christmas. It's for the evening news." She looked him up and down. "Maria thought you'd be good to interview. D'you fancy answering a few questions on camera?"

Of course, the natural answer would have been to tell this impudent girl to get lost, and to point out how blasted rude it is to talk to people while listening to music, but for some reason Warren found himself saying, "Yes. OK."

"Good." Parka girl grabbed his sleeve and pulled him over to sweater girl, who he presumed was this all-powerful Maria.

Parka girl raised her clipboard and poised her pen.

"Your name?"

"Warren Pierce. P-I-E,..."

"Yeah, yeah, got it," she interrupted, scribbling on her pad. "Stand here." She moved him next to the cameraman, opposite Maria.

Warren was acutely aware that he was now the centre of attention for the crowd. He kept his gaze on Maria and tried to block out the many eyes he knew were scrutinising him from all sides. Then he became aware that Maria was speaking not to the camera, but directly to him.

"Some people believe that the meaning of Christmas has been completely lost to commercialisation," she told him. "What do you think this means for the residents of Wycombe?" Then she laughed. "I meant Windsor! Sorry, very silly of me – Wycombe was yesterday." She resumed her serious expression. "Can we go again?" The cameraman nodded. Maria repeated the question, correctly this time, then paused and asked, "That okay?" The cameraman nodded again, then shuffled round and pointed the lens directly at Warren. The sound man held the microphone somewhere near his crotch, pointing upwards like a small dog begging for a scrap.

Warren looked past the deep black lens to Maria, who repeated the question one more time, finishing with a smile and a small wave of her hand to suggest he should now give his answer.

A red light appeared above the lens. For a moment Warren struggled, as if his tongue had become superglued to the roof of his mouth.

Then he had a moment of absolute clarity.

He had opinions.

On Christmas. On commercialisation. He had cogent, reasoned arguments on just these topics which he frequently aired at dinner parties. And here he was, with a nationwide, possibly global, audience, waiting to hear what he had to say. He cleared his throat.

"Let me tell you exactly what I think…" he began.

*****

A few minutes later, Warren was back on his way home, still clutching his cardboard box. He felt as if he was floating above the ground, wafting along on a euphoric cloud of wonderful approval. Yes, he had been lucid. Yes, he had been compelling. He had looked Maria in the eyes and told her, in no uncertain terms, exactly how things were.

She had nodded. Smiled. She had agreed with every point he had made. She hadn't tutted, rolled her eyes, or grimaced like his wife and daughters – no, she had truly got it. He could see that. Every nuanced little part of it; she had just darn-well got it.

As she'd said after he'd finished, it was an 'awesome piece'. A definite for the evening news. Imagine that – Warren Pierce giving his considered views on the evening news!

He stopped as a thought came to him. He'd be seen giving weighty, well-thought-out opinions on nuanced topics. Thinking like that was valued. People with something valid to say were always in demand. He'd probably get invited onto serious art shows now. Or even political discussions.

"So, Warren, what's your view on the latest literary novel?"

"Well, Melvyn, I am glad you asked me that…"

"Does the Government deserve re-election, Mr. Pierce?"

"That's a great question, Laura; let's take an in-depth look…"

Should he get an agent?

On that happy thought he resumed his journey home.

*****

After supper, the Pierce household settled in front of the evening news in a state of high excitement. At least Warren was excited; Julie's interest seemed guarded, and the girls were more absorbed by their iPhones than the prospect of their father appearing on TV.

The main news finished. Warren shushed everyone through a couple of uninspiring stories about local businesses, then Maria came on screen in her cream sweater.

"That's her! This is it!"

Reluctantly the girls peered over the tops of their phones, while Julie held her breath and surreptitiously crossed her fingers.

"There are those who say the true meaning of Christmas has been lost. Indeed, Christmas is no longer a religious festival, but a purely commercial one." Maria paused as the picture cut to shoppers on Peascod Street. "I am here in the Queen's back yard, in the town of Windsor, to see what the local shoppers think."

Warren's face filled the screen.

"Is there something wrong with your tongue, dear?" asked Julie. "It looks like it's stuck to your mouth."

Then the picture cut back to Maria. "Some people believe that the meaning of Christmas has been completely lost to commercialisation," she asked. "What do you think this means for the residents of Windsor?"

There was a pause, then a caption came up on the screen below Warren.

'Warren Peace, Windsor Resident.'

"They've got your name wrong, dad," observed Sophie.

The on-screen Warren said, "In a commercial society, shopping is the only true religion and buying gifts at Christmas is the necessary way to observe that religion."

The off-screen Warren was ominously silent.

Maria gave a shallow smile. "Very interesting. Thanks for that," she said. "Now back to the studio."

Warren was still silent, although Julie noted that his face was going progressively redder, and it looked like he was now holding his breath.

Sophie was busy tapping on her screen. "Maria Coleman, 32," she said. "She's got over forty thousand followers on Instagram. Her fingers were suddenly still. "Oh…" She stared at the screen. After a minute she handed the phone to Lucy, who bit her lip as she watched, then handed it on to Julie.

"Warren Peace?!" shouted Warren suddenly, making Sophie jump and Lucy drop her phone. "Warren bloody Peace?!" He fought for breath, his mouth opening and closing like a goldfish.

"Isn't that a TV series, dad?" asked Lucy. "War and Peace?"

"I'll get you a nice cup of tea, dear," said Julie, handing the phone back to Sophie with a small shake of her head, as if to say, "Better keep this quiet."

"I don't want any bloody tea!" shouted Warren. "Warren bloody Peace!"

He glared at his family. "And they only used one sentence. One sentence! I said a lot more! Lots! Good stuff about the power of corporations and the acquiescence of the Church, and the state of the decorations in Windsor. I gave them way more than that one measly sentence.

"I know you did, dad," said Sophie. She looked at Julie who gave a 'I suppose he'll find out sooner or later…' shrug. "The full interview is all over Instagram. It's been set to music as a rap, with the caption: 'Warren Peace – just like War and Peace, he goes on and on and on…' She held the phone up and Warren watched in silence, his face reddening more than Julie had ever seen as he stared at the screen.

Then he crumpled, falling back into the sofa like a deflating beach ball.

"I'm ruined," he whispered.

*****

The cardboard box sat forgotten on the hall table.

It was two days before Warren noticed it and took it up to his study. Like an automaton who has no understanding of its actions, he opened it with a pair of scissors and shook the contents onto his desk. He stared at the small plush stuffed rabbit for nearly a minute, before he fished out the delivery note and gazed blankly at it.

Julie put her head round the door. "You really do have to let it go, Warren..." she began, then she noticed the rabbit. "What's that?"

"It's a stuffed rabbit."

"Who for?"

"Lucy."

"Lucy?"

"That's what I said."

"But she wanted a Glamour Puss cat doll, not a rabbit. She's been going on about getting a Glamour Puss for weeks. It's been driving me mad."

"I know. I ordered a Glamour Puss." He held up the note. "It says here 'One Glamour Puss'. But in the parcel, one stuffed rabbit."

Julie pulled a face. "She really is set on a Glamour Puss. Apparently, several girls in her class have got one and she's absolutely desperate. Can you send it back?"

"Of course," he replied in a dull voice. "But tomorrow's Christmas Eve. There's no way they can send me a Glamour Puss in time."

"Oh. You'll have to go to the shops in Windsor and see if you can get one."

Warren looked up from the rabbit. "Go out?" he asked, his voice still dull. "See people?" He swallowed hard. "And presumably be laughed at?"

"Don't be silly. Who's going to laugh at you?" replied Julie, but even to her it sounded hollow. "It'll do you good to get out. Get some fresh air after two days stuck inside."

"That video," Warren observed, "was shared more than one and a half million times."

Julie bit her lip. "Actually, it's over two million now."

"Whatever," Warren muttered.

He clutched the rabbit to his chest. "If it's been shared that many times, it's likely everyone in Windsor has seen it."

Julie put on a bright smile. "Not everyone, surely?"

"Everyone."

Julie took his free hand. "Warren, love, you'll have to go out sometime. And Lucy really, really wants a Glamour Puss…"

Warren looked up at her with big eyes, like a smacked puppy.

"If you don't go out now, you never will."

Warren stood, carefully placed the rabbit back in the box, and put on his coat.

The air outside was clear and bright as he stepped into Fountain Gardens and started walking slowly into the town centre, heading for the big store with its extensive toy department.

Eventually he arrived. Heading for the girls' toy section, he looked for the distinctive pink Glamour Puss packaging and the image of a female-bodied doll with its over made-up cat-like head. Once at the fixture, however, there was no sign of it.

Which meant he'd have to ask.

"Excuse me, do you have any Glamour Puss dolls?" he whispered to an assistant.

"Sorry, sir. Didn't catch that."

Warren cleared his throat. "Do you have any Glamour Puss dolls?" he repeated louder.

"Ah, no, sorry. We're all sold out…" The assistant faltered to a stop, frowning at him. Then it was as if a light of recognition came on in her eyes, and she said, "You're him! You're that local Windsor man, 'War and Peace'!" She rocked her head side to side in silent mirth: "Goes on and on and on and on!" She seemed oblivious to Warren's granite stare. "Hope we're not being too commercial for you at Christmas!"

"Not if you don't have any Glamour Puss dolls," observed Warren, before walking out of the store.

He made his way to another shop that sold a range of books and toys.

"Do you have any Glamour Puss…" he began as he walked in, but the assistant was already staring at him in wide-eyed recognition. "War and Peace!" she shrieked, thumping her fellow worker in the ribs with her elbow. "It's War and Peace! Look! It's him!"

"Eh?" said the other assistant, staring at Warren. "So it is," he said. "Goes on and on and on and on!" He chuckled. "Loved it!"

Warren took a breath to steady himself. "Do you have," he asked, making sure every word was clear, "any Glamour Puss dolls?"

"Oh," said the first assistant. "No, sorry. Sold out."

"Right," said Warren, and he left the shop, with their laughter following him out into the street.

Three more shops followed, and in each he was subjected to the same ridicule, and informed that the Glamour Puss doll range had completely sold out. "Very popular," he was told each time, "This year's 'must have' for the kids," as well as variations on the theme that as an anti-commercialist, he shouldn't be trying to buy the most popular toy.

He stopped outside his favourite coffee shop. How nice it had been in happier times, to relax over a cappuccino and grab a few minutes of calm in the middle of his frenetic schedule. But now he shuddered at the thought of sitting in full view and suffering the ridicule of yet more strangers. These were people who thought they knew him, but only knew one thing – that he had been made to look a fool on social media. Quickly he walked on.

Finally, he went back into the toy department of the first store.

"I would like to see the manager," he said to the sniggering sales assistant.

"You won't be going on and on and on and on if I get her?"

"No, I won't," Warren answered, trying to control his urge to scream obscenities, pull toys off the shelf and throw them across
the store. "I have a question I need to ask her."

The assistant went over to the sales desk and spoke with an older lady, glancing back and pointing at Warren, her shoulders shaking and a broad smile on her face. He watched as the older lady responded without any glee, and as she talked, the smile faded from the assistant's face, her shoulders stilled, and she hung her head in shame.

The older lady then marched over to Warren.

"I must apologise, sir, for any inappropriate behaviour. Some of my staff are young, and easily influenced by what they see on their phones. If you wish to complain…?"

Warren paused. It would be very satisfying to complain – not just about this assistant, but about all the people in all the shops who had been so ready to make fun of him.

But…

He shook his head. What would it achieve? Would it right the wrong he had suffered? Or would it just confirm that Maria Coleman (32) had been correct on her social media post, and in truth he was just a pompous little man who went 'on and on and on and on?'

Then Warren saw clearly what this whole thing had been.

It had been a wake-up call – a lesson to him to try to be a little more understanding; a little more forgiving; a little kinder to those around him.

He looked at the manager, who was standing calmly in front of him. She had treated him fairly, and had not judged him as a social media victim, but as a wronged customer. She embodied the kindness that Christmas should really be all about.

"No, I have no wish to complain," he answered.

She nodded. "Then how can I be of help?"

"My daughter has set her heart on a Glamour Puss doll. I have searched Windsor top to bottom, and they are all sold out. I wondered if you might have some tucked away in the stock room?" Warren paused hopefully, "I would be immensely grateful."

The woman nodded again, as if this was what she was hoping to hear. "I'll see what I can do to help. Let me go and check."

While she was gone, Warren looked around. He definitely spotted a few glances in his direction; a few small sniggers; a few quick head-turns away. But what did it matter? Let them have their fun.

A couple of minutes later the woman reappeared.

With a pink box under her arm.

Warren very nearly leapt forward and kissed her, but as she handed it over, he limited himself to a warm smile and a heartfelt, "Thank you."

"There was an unopened carton of stock that got overlooked," she explained. "I hope your daughter likes it."

"She will. Thanks again."

Emerging back into the street clutching his prize, Warren found himself once again outside his favourite coffee shop.

"Why the heck not?" he said aloud, pushed open the door and went inside.

2
Beyond Repair
By Adrian McBreen

On the shortest day of the year, they'd be getting more sunlight. A morning westbound transatlantic flight meant an extension of that annual marker's rays by a few extra hours.

The solstice was always a special day for Joshua, a sacrosanct time just before the true seasonal madness kicked in, when he was reminded of more important things than fake snow, mountains of plastic waste, inane "festive" muzak and enforced joviality. He seemed to be the only member of his household to whom this cyclical clock actually mattered; astronomy, nature, mystery, and magic all rolled into one.

He had followed the hordes to Stonehenge in June most years, but it was the midwinter festival that struck a chord in his heart. The monoliths have a firm place on the tourist trail from London along with Windsor and Bath, which offer their own heritage delights.

For the first time he'd miss his late night pilgrimage to Wiltshire, yet he still stood at the bus stop on St Leonard's Road in inky pre-dawn light. Only that morning he would be meeting his parents a full four hours before their flight in the December chaos of Heathrow Terminal 5. "Better to be early for these international flights than rush through security," said his mother. He rolled his eyes and glanced at his father, as the capitalist euphemism 'shopping opportunities' – so thinly veiled it was almost transparent – flashed up on the departure information screens.

Silent plasma TV screens next to the gate showed morning news bulletins. A scrolling banner read: 'Crowds gather at

Stonehenge to mark winter solstice' while images of golden sunlight piercing over the heel stone repeated on a loop. Smiling groups in heavy winter coats, beanie hats and scarves were huddled around inside the circle; their faces aglow as light slowly shone. He recognised some of them as fellow solstice hunters.

That day should've been the end of the world, apparently. An ancient Mayan prophecy had foreseen it over two thousand years ago, as their mathematical calculations, combined with a 'portentous' alignment of the date's calendar figures meant certain doom. Conspiracy theorists and crackpot apocalypse fanatics had hyped the big day for decades, citing the date, 21/12/2012 as evidence of certain Armageddon. Was it just a cosmic kink in time or evidence of something far more profound? He plumped for the former. Humanity survived and our world kept turning. The morning's astronomical light show only heralded humanity's continuation as a species. A chain of natural disasters like massive tidal waves, global earthquakes or volcanic eruptions hadn't wiped us out.

The sun's return after the longest night had been celebrated for millennia. It was no different that morning. But looking back, maybe it was an omen, a sign from the gods, of the troubled waters that lay in wait across the pond.

Joshua counted his blessings. One missed winter solstice wouldn't hurt; even a rare cloudless sky that morning wouldn't dampen his spirits. The prospect of a US holiday away from the usual festive routine appealed. Plus, he'd get to spend some quality time with his parents.

And then of course there was his filial American wing, to which 'family time' was nauseatingly reinforced. At Christmas, those levels would be ramped up by around a thousand.

They landed at O'Hare two hours late because of a de-icing back in London. Rachel, his sister, met them in arrivals with a wide smile. They all walked outside through large revolving doors; instantly the freezing air hit them like a volley of tiny daggers. Her shiny grey minivan, around which snow had already begun to accumulate, sat in the middle of a vast car park.

They got inside faster than starving hobos at a free all-you-can-eat buffet.

She drove out on the freeway, and almost immediately landed in deepest suburbia. Tree-lined roads where houses of an oddly similar style, most sporting clapboard porches and mock Tudor frames, stood behind whiteout lawns. There were Obama-Biden signs planted in them while obligatory Stars and Stripes fluttered over windows and garages. Each house was framed by an open perimeter of snow-cleared concrete slabs. It looked as if the residents were searching for some tiny scrap of individuality, in which their house would somehow stand out amongst a bland sea of uniformity.

He had arranged to stay with his brother, James, and sister in-law, Kellie, at their home closer to the city. Their house was straight out of a Pottery Barn catalogue, all sturdy wooden furniture, throw pillows, clean drapes, fruit-bowls, and ornamental coffee table art books. Is there anything less essential than essential oils? It was in a sought-after residential area full of quiet streets, with unfeasibly large houses squeezed tightly into individual plots. The homely feel was an effect of maximising every space to get the most real estate value out of each property.

James had gone native in recent years; he'd become a fat, brash, obnoxious yank and met the stereotypes of his adopted homeland with bells and whistles. Kellie was a former Miss Idaho, homecoming queen, star cheerleader and girl next door; she ticked every box on the all-American checklist: blonde, semi-professional, attractive, well-spoken, upwardly mobile and a waspish card-carrying Republican. She was the perfect trophy wife for an ambitious go-getter immigrant on the make.

Their ten-year-old wanted to visit Medieval Times; not exactly top of Joshua's list, but it was Christmas, a time when 'family' became oh so important. He duly piled in with James, Kellie and their three rugrats for the drive to a dreary suburb. The nearest gaudy homage to medieval history lay just off the I-90. An enormous US flag stood on the front entrance, barely fluttering due to the frigid air and its sheer weight. It seemed to be announcing, to Joshua at least, that the wild anachronisms and mock anarchy on display inside would be grossly simplified, Americanised to the nth degree and should be taken with a large bucketful of salt. The building was surrounded by a low-rise urban sprawl of fast-food restaurants, chain supermarkets, home improvement warehouses and vast car parks.

The building looked like a child's Lego recreation of a medieval castle, all linear cream walls, evenly spaced turrets, rounded ramparts, and arrow shaped windows. Being faced with that manufactured, sanitised version of a medieval castle was slightly ironic, especially when he had a real-life, working example back in Windsor. Inside the castellated foyer there were flags, shields, crests, suits of armour and generic period maps of Europe and, bizarrely, the US, hung on walls. As this was America, the whole experience was centred on food.

Patrons were each given a colour and family crest to support during the night's 'dinner and tournament' inside the arena. Performers on horseback would re-enact medieval jousting matches while audiences feasted on beef strips, chicken legs, potatoes, and pie, washed down by copious amounts of mead and ale. This translated as burgers, fries, nachos, and beer. They ate from metal dishes, although it was permissible to use cutlery, scooping with their bare hands was clearly a step too far in historical accuracy. Diners could bellow 'wench', 'fusty lugs', 'scallion' and 'low-born hobgoblin' to insult each other with giddy 21st century abandon.

Staying at Kellie and James's show-home meant he could experience the 'joy' of Medieval Times and spend time with one side of his American family. It was important to share the love between both overseas families whenever he was in town. He'd spend time with the other expat wing of his family at Rachel's place in suburbia.

But Joshua had one more night with the city power couple, Christmas Eve-eve. Kellie and James had invited him and his parents, who had been staying out with Rachel and her lot, to dinner at a restaurant downtown. The plan would be for him and his parents to go back to Rachel's place the next day.

The cavernous Italian restaurant was next to the hotel where James had booked a suite for their parents as a surprise. The conversation revolved almost entirely around James's stunning financial successes. "Looks like December's gonna be my best month ever, I've already closed on three-million-dollar houses on the North Shore. And probably another one sold next week with a bit of luck." He said this before barking at an unfortunate waitress because his penne weren't quite al dente enough. "Take it back and bring me another!"

It was after that exchange of white privilege that Joshua left the table. He couldn't listen to another sermon on economics and entitlement from his brother without a yuletide fraternal argument. His brother had always been superior, but it seemed to have ballooned into a full-on messiah complex. Be careful, James, lest you suffer vertigo from dizzying heights up on your moral ground. He excused himself. Those ten minutes were all it took for his sister-in-law to lob her grenade, its fuse primed for a spark before it blew.

When Joshua returned to their table, a stony silence quickly enveloped the group. The atmosphere of a cosy holiday family dinner had, while he was away for a matter of minutes, completely frosted over. It was like the hatch in a pressurised air lock had been flung open, its oxygen-rich air rapidly sucked out into deep space. Any one of them could've picked up a knife and slashed the tension. The silence he returned to was not only uncomfortable, but it was also excruciating. Something had happened. Kellie had made an insensitive comment again. His temporary absence had presented her with an opportunity to say something about God knows what. His brother had gone white as a sheet, while his parents had stunned eyes widened; Kellie's eyes, on the other hand, were glazed.

After dinner they got a taxi up along the lakeshore back to the house; everything seemed normal, nothing amiss. Apart from that weird moment of dead air at the table, it was just another pre-Christmas night out with family. Once back at Hipsterville, he had a nightcap of some Irish whiskies with Kellie and James at the kitchen island. His bed was a huge corner couch in the basement, or 'man cave,' which was dominated by a massive plasma TV.

*****

In the morning he packed his bag, said a warm goodbye to Kellie and the kids at the front porch. "Thanks guys, see you all tomorrow" – they'd all spend Christmas Day together out at Rachel's place. He took a train back downtown to meet his parents, called his father from the front desk and made his way up to their huge room. That's when the proverbial began to hit the fan.

It was one of those dazzling winter mornings with barely a breath of wind and clear blue skies. A frozen stillness in the air compacted overnight snow, large chunks of flat ice clung to the lakefront like crazy paving. His father sat at the end of the bed and his mother slid a heavily laden breakfast tray away from her propped position. She said: "Go on, tell us, we want to know exactly what went on in that house with those two." Joshua looked at his father, then to his mother. "Kellie told us you 'treated the place like a hotel' apparently and came and went as you pleased. She also mentioned something about scrambled eggs, you didn't wash up after breakfast; your bed wasn't made; you didn't greet her properly."

At first, he thought it was a joke and chuckled. "First of all: I am on holiday; they have a dishwasher; I was sleeping on the couch, so could only fold bed linen; and she was asleep when I arrived." A quick glance at his father confirmed Kellie's grievances were genuine. "Is that what the silence was about when I came back from the lav? I knew she must've said something."

He was just as confused as they were. "Seriously, I have no idea what she's talking about. She's totally mental. Why would she try to confront you two anyway? Couldn't she just have spoken to me directly like a normal person? What a two-faced bitch, and involving you two in this is so insulting. Does she have any sense?" He didn't want to make a knee-jerk reaction though. Presumably, she'd been bitching about him to all and sundry for years. A phone call to Kellie would keep this simmering pot from boiling over; nip this weed in the bud before it spread.

It was a commuter terminal station, all glass and chrome steel set back from the street. There was a forty-minute wait until their train. Joshua called her from a high stool outside one of the many cafés lining the concourse. "Kellie. I hear you have some complaints," he opened the discussion. "We always got on well, one of the better in-laws in this family, despite your wildly passive aggressive streak. I was willing to overlook that for the sake of family. I want to know one thing: why on earth did you go behind my back with this? What possessed you?"

She paused for a long time, white noise crackling on the line. In her infuriatingly calm tone, "I did it to improve your relationship with your brother."

"How noble of you! If you wanted to fix it, you've just torpedoed it."

*****

Joshua and his parents arrived at Revolutionary Road, the tinder of Kellie's twisted third-party intervention raw. But their tale was music to the ears of one person at least. Rachel, whose friendship with Kellie was always about as welcome as that between lampposts and dogs, reacted with righteous indignation and anger. When she heard of her sister-in-law's latest faux pas she leapt straight into that pot and stirred; she saw the kindling, doused the pile with a jerry can full of petrol, flicked a lit match right into its core and watched the inferno. "I think we should cancel tomorrow; she's upset you all too much this time. Who gave her the right to 'fix' you and James anyway?"

James, loaded up on happy pills, drove to the suburbs the next day, Christmas Day, alone with the presents they had planned to exchange together. Rachel wasn't surprised: "I mean, what did she think was going to happen?"

*****

It turned out, Kellie and James filed for divorce soon after that unseemly episode. So, who knows: maybe it was the beginning of the end or just the end of the beginning? Was that Christmas the thin end of the wedge?

James had had an affair with his secretary for the previous six years. The people at Christmas are far more important than the date.

3
Beldame
By Helena Marie

Somewhere around these parts, my ancestor was hanged. It must have been a grand day out, for a pamphlet was made, and people came from Ascot and Dedworth and all hereabouts to watch her swing from this earth into the care of Our Lord (though most said Old Nick was her master). I never met the woman, for this took place before my mother's mother, before a time of horse and carriage and carrying slopping buckets upstairs to Mistress and her complaints, yet I knew the crime ran through me. This hag, whose blood was in my veins was, by all accounts, given to shrewing and not doing anybody's bidding but her own, yet for all that, she was wise: a cunning woman of herbs and hedgelore. She knew her place, and even with their gossip, people would come to have the hex made gone or something to calm a fever. Still, there's wanted and there's needed, and she was none of one and some of the other. We had that in common too.

From my earliest beginnings, naked on the beaten earth, I knew that I was tainted. Oh, it was all very well for mam to laugh away the stares of strangers, but little people know things, and this one heard well enough that she was damned. Bad blood runs deep they say, and in my case, it was deeper than most. Still, I grew to be a passable child, not plain, yet not fair of face, but with a pert manner sharpened by wits. I could cut a purse and be gone before it was even reached for, and when it was, I'd be eating scraps by the castle. So it was that cunning was my way, my keep paid for by thieving, and in this manner, we went on. But it didn't last. Once numbers had been learnt and chalk scratched on slate, mam looked to put me out to learn a servant's trade she said, but I knew she wanted my bed, to earn a penny for the night.

"But I don't want to go, I want to stay here."

"Child, it is time to make your way. There's bare food enough for one and you bring me nothing but trouble with your thieving and your lies."

"I can do better mam, I can. I'll find some work and get more food and things can be as they are now."

"That kind of work will bring men and trouble to my door. No child, there's nothing for it, leave you must, and soon."

"Where? Where can I go? I got no papers, no skills, no one will have me. I'm better off here with you."

"No, my mind is made up. Tomorrow I'll take you to the big houses and we'll see what we can find."

*****

I didn't hold the promise that she'd hoped for though; my situations withered and died, for I still had restless hands and eyes that were caught by glitter. Nothing greedy, mind, just small tokens that no one of their sort should miss: a trinket cut from glass, a pretty piece of cotton. But missed they were, and I was to learn the hard way that a trifle is wanted more than a maid, and a new situation is hard to find for a cursed child without her papers. The gallows could have called for me, but mam got wind of a house that couldn't keep maids on account of the work, so I was told to mend my ways and muster what little charm I had and was sent to the yard to meet a puff-faced virago who called herself Cook.

"She don't look like much of a scrap. Not no use for nothing," were the first words she spoke and not even to me, but to a skinny looking fellow wiping down a horse.

"Looks like a good wind would snap her," was his reply and I struggled to keep a nice word on my tongue for I would have liked to snap both of them, but remembering mam, I tried my best to be polite.

"I may not have papers but I'm stronger than I look and mighty willing to work hard – harder than most if I may say so," I ventured.

"May you now? And how would you be proving that? This ain't no slack house you know."

"I can scrub and clean and lift heavy things and I ain't the sickly kind neither," I said, with perhaps a little too much tartness.

"Looks sickly enough to me," the man said under his breath, but loud enough that I heard it anyway.

"Don't mind him, he's not all in his head. Can you carry coals and make a fire? Do you know how to address a Lady?"

"I do and what I don't know you can be sure I'll learn in no time. I'm keen, that's what I am, and I can start today, if you say so."

"Well, you either will or you won't but maybe we'll find out soon enough; I take my orders from Mistress and no one else. You wait here and I'll see what's to be done."

I watched her go inside and wondered how it would be if I too lived here, maid of all work, and master of none. The man stared at me, but I ignored him and thought he'd get a good putting in his place if I ever got the chance. There wasn't long to wait before she came back, a resigned look on her great big face, and said "You can go inside, Mistress is to try you out for one week but if you ain't up to it you'll be back out bothering someone else, make no mistake."

This is how I came to be baking and scrubbing and blacking by day, and shiver-sleeping for never long enough in my moonlit room, as much outdoors as in by the taunting draught. Those dark hours, waiting for the balm of hard-won slumber, I knew in my bones there was bad in me, that my forebear's ways would be my own, and slowly, like reluctant fire, my destiny unfurled.

It was the little things that started it: the curdled milk when I was in my monthlies, the dead hen after a fair cussing out, bread gone stale too soon because my hands had made it. Mistress saw my sins and said my arse would know the street again before too long, or summat in that vein. Like I said though, I had wits and lived on them, so I soothed and cried and swore to do better and every time, my foolish Lady believed me.

Time ran past me as a stream by a tree; my hands made chapped by scrubbing and soaking and peeling and fetching, and my back so sore that water spilled when I tried to lift it. This was my lot, to be borne with a reigned-in mouth and a gratitude I didn't feel. So, when the horse slipped on cobbles and gave the Young Misses a fright – for they were in the cab – it was me to blame for its lameness.

"If she had made the poultice right, its leg would have healed," I heard Cook telling the Groom (that being the name skin-and-bones gave himself).

"I told you she was wrong. I told you from the day she came here. No box, no papers. I knew she was no good."

"You'll have to tell her. You're in charge of the horses, it's your job this time."

I was sent to the stable yard and told my luck was nearly out; one more mistake and Mistress would be glad to see me gone. A calmer head than mine would have been a blessing but it wasn't one I had, so I told the Groom if he had done his job, I wouldn't be blamed for doing mine, and was I to do all the work so he could do less? Well, that set him off on a proper rant and a cursing like that I would have been proud of myself, but like most fights it sounded worse than it was, and I went to bed knowing that by daybreak he'd be more interested in the bottle than in me.

Things went on with all the ways of a household and its staff, and soon enough the Young Misses outgrew their home, and each found some chap with a place of his own to take her in, no doubt tormenting servants in their new names, as this household got smaller, and my work grew lighter. I was in about my 18th year by now and as settled as I'd ever been. Mistress had softened a little with the years, widow's weeds coming to suit her, and when one day she called to see me, she was almost kind.

"It's a sorry day when news likes this is brought to one so alone in the world."

I didn't know what she meant so I asked, "Is it the horse, Mistress? Did I do something wrong?"

"No dear, not the horse. It's your mother. I'm sorry. She's made a journey, and she won't be coming back."

Well, I had no idea of what she meant and living by wits is a hard habit to break so I thought I could make some advantage of this.

"Is she gone far then, Mistress?"

"Child, you misunderstand. Your poor mother was taken."

I had feelings for my mam, but I wasn't a child and she had thrown me out anyway so I couldn't help but play my hand a little harder.

"Taken? That's terrible. Do you know where they took her?"

"Who girl? Who took her where?"

"I don't know, Mistress. Isn't that what you were telling me?"

"Child, your mother is dead, and gone to meet her maker."

If tears could catch me unawares at any time, this was it, so I pouted my lip and sniffed like Groom before he hacked one up, and cried partly for effect but mostly because then I knew she really was gone, and for better or worse, she was all I'd had in the world.

*****

Seasons changed and planting turned to digging up, foraging to fire making, until December was upon us again. That winter was a harsh one: water froze in the pails and the yard was treacherous with ice; I could see my words as they left me in the biting air. We toiled to keep fires stoked and hearths alight, running ragged in pursuit of ourselves for even still there was more work than hands to do it.

And so, you see, the terrible day was not my fault.

It was a bitter, foggy one and Cook and the Groom were coming to blows at where to put the big spruce tree – Prince Albert's pointless fancy if you asked me, but that was of no consequence to anyone – the heaving and dragging of it carried on anyway. What with helping Cook and running between the yard and house, I was in all places at once but never where I was needed, so it can't be laid at my feet that an ember must surely have jumped from hearth to rug, and everybody being too concerned with the stupid tree and the endless food, it can only have smoked and smouldered its way into proper danger. No matter, the fighting carried on and I had no business to be standing still indoors when there was work to do, and so between us we busied ourselves in a house that was settled on not needing it.

The tree having found its rightful place – in the hall, by the stairs for anyone minded to care – Cook set to salvaging whatever she could on the range, and the Groom no doubt made new acquaintance with the wine. Mistress must have rung, for my name was being called from the kitchen. The back stairs were as gloomy as ever they were at wintertime, yet still, there was a dullness and odour to them that wasn't right. I was halfway up to see for what she was calling when, I know not why, my inner senses told me turn around. That's when a shadow of smoke stole from beneath the door. Well, I didn't need showing twice – I was back downstairs, and hand on handle to the hall before you could say a word, but the door was hot and that wasn't right, so I shouted for Cook, all the while fearing that what I knew was true: something was afire. Panic took my heart; my thinking was all gone, and everything met me in a chaos of terror and instinct. My hand paining me from the hotness, I gave one sharp turn, and the door gave in to a heat like I'd never felt, and brightness; so much light I had to look away. It took many blinks for the stinging to leave my eyes and the flames and awfulness to make themselves real, yet like an idiot I stood gaping into the hall until the fire touched the door frame, and then, without a second thought, I turned, took heel, and ran.

"Where in God's name do you think you're going? Get back here at once! Get back here if you know what's good for you..."

Cook's shouting meant nothing to me. I was quick on my feet and flames and distance soon silenced her, and nothing she said could have changed my mind anyway.

Away from the yelling noise, my ears filled instead with cracking and splitting, and the choking air wrapped itself around my lungs, so I couldn't breathe natural but gasped in and out as I tried to find a way around it, but it was growing thicker as I ran and I knew that if I didn't move faster than I ever had, I wouldn't get away. My strength was almost gone, but with a few more breaths the air started to clear, and I could see my way to where I needed to be, and come what may, I knew I'd made my choice. Almost falling, I leant against the wall to regain myself, and then, when my feet would move as I bade them; I lunged forward not knowing what was before me, or where I might end.

*****

43

It was many days before I stood again in the yard and saw what little was left. Even still there was some small warmth from the charred beams, and the air all sour from smoke. Here and there a piece of furniture, sodden from water buckets hurled over everything; nothing that would be worth taking space again. Not that Mistress had a need for any of that now.

Standing a while, I dared myself to remember, to know it as it was. Cook had given me up for lost and shouted for the Groom and between their clamour others had come to wrestle with the flames and try to stop the spread, but I was not among them.

I, with my so-called evil blood and thieving ways, had run as if life depended on it, for I had fled not from the house, but further in, and in that blaze, I saw my true self and knew I could not leave.

So it was that I alone brought my Mistress out, her half demented with fear and crying, but brought her out I did, to a lost world and a new life cleansed by fire: everything gone, and nothing left but new beginnings. And in doing that for her, I did the same for me.

4
Festive Spirit
By Wendy Gregory

Crikey, it's cold today! That wind is whipping round the castle, chasing people down the street without mercy. Nope, the weather doesn't pick and choose; it harasses the young, the old, the thin, the fat, the rich and the poor alike, causing everyone to hunch their shoulders up and pull their scarves a little tighter around their necks, to quicken their pace or nip inside a shop, allegedly to browse. Can't blame them for that. I do it myself often, rifling through the glittering racks of clothes, special outfits for office parties or maybe for the big day itself. I don't have any parties planned this year myself, but I still like to think it could happen. You never know, I might get a sudden surprise invitation from Her Majesty. After all, we live on the same street!

It's four o'clock, already dark and the shops will be closing soon. After popping into McDonald's for a coffee (okay, I know, so non-U, but right now I can't stretch to The Castle Hotel, or even Costa), I decide to have a wander down Peascod Street. The anticipation is palpable; tomorrow is Christmas Day. It's magical – frantic yummy mummies heading towards Waitrose for their forgotten goose fat or vegan gravy, urging Luke and Lucinda to "Hurry up darlings, the shops are closing soon," whilst their still-believing offspring, wide eyed and warmly wrapped up, press their noses up against Daniel's window, gazing at the display. This year it's all about The Nutcracker: huge tin soldiers standing to attention and the Sugar Plum Fairy in a glittering tutu. I sigh. Those were the days, Mummy used to take us to the ballet every Boxing Day.

I decide to have a little look inside. It's not Harvey Nicks but it does have some rather gorgeous handbags. Whilst fondling a particularly attractive pale pink one in nubuck leather, as soft and silky as a well-fed cat, I notice a shop assistant behind me. "Can I help you madam?" As I turn to face her, she looks me up and down, struggling to hide her contempt.

"No thank you dear, I'm just browsing. I need a new handbag, don't you think?" We both look down at the grubby, bulging holdall I'm clutching, complete with broken zip and fraying handles. "The problem is we ladies tend to overfill our bags, don't we?" She takes a step back and clears her throat, surprised; a common occurrence as my accent is at odds with my clothing, which has seen better days. Much better.

"Is it okay?" I ask.

"Is what okay?" She seems all discombobulated.

"For me to browse?"

"Oh yes. Of course, Madam. But we will be closing in ten minutes."

"No problem. I hope you have a lovely Christmas," I beam at her as I turn back to the handbag stand. I intend to stay as long as I possibly can, keen to avoid going back out into the cold.

Ultimately, of course, back out I go. It's quieter now outside, just a few desperate looking men, no doubt hubbies hoping they'll find somewhere still open so they can get something for their wives. Why do they always leave it to the last minute? Oh well, some things don't change.

I saunter back up through King Edward Court, more for the shelter it offers against the wind than for anything else, but on the spur of the moment I decide to take a quick look at Alexandra Gardens, throw a penny into the fountains opposite and make a wish. Silly superstition I know, but we bear the same name, the gardens and I. Eyelids squeezed tightly together, in goes the coin and I wish, "Bring joy to the world, let everyone have something to be glad for this Christmas and please let next year be different in however small a way. Let me have just one little bit of luck!" Now I know all too well that regrets are pointless (and heaven knows I have enough of them); the past is done. But it's tough when you just can't see a future. I turn and cross the road.

Everything is closing – the pop-up ice rink is pretty deserted apart from a couple of workers tidying up and putting everything away, switching off the power, anxious to get home to their mince pies and mulled wine no doubt. Just as I'm about to go back up to the High Street one of them calls, "Hey love, would you like some of these?" My eyesight is so poor I can't see what he's holding, but then I can smell it, fried onions, spices, and alcohol. I step closer and see he's offering me a box containing a hotdog, mince pies and a paper cup of mulled cider. I salivate. "That's very kind of you my dear. Come to think of it, I am a little peckish."

"It'll only be thrown out otherwise. Let me put it in a bag for you." He brings a now bulging white paper bag over to me. "Merry Christmas, love. You stay warm now."

Well, I reflect, perhaps my luck has changed after all. My step is somewhat brisker as I head back to the castle, where a few families are staring up at the round tower with its enchanting holographic light display. I reach my front door. Fortunately, mine is set back from the pavement, providing some shelter from the wind. I get settled in it for the night, pulling my sleeping bag up around me and covering it with a layer of bin bags for extra insulation.

I am just starting to doze when something catches my eye. Emerging from Charlotte Street by the castle and turning into the High Street are two police officers. There's nothing unusual about that, of course, but I don't recognise them; they aren't our usual community Bobbies, with whom I am on first-name terms. The woman is very tall with a long, elegant stride; as they cross the road and come towards me, I see the man is dark-skinned and struggling to keep pace with her. "Good evening, madam," says the female officer. She looks at me with piercing, but strangely familiar blue eyes. Her gaze is as straight and direct as the arrow from a crossbow.

"Have you just been on duty outside the castle?" I reply. "I don't envy you, it's really rather parky out here today."

She chuckles and says, "Not exactly. I was just checking in with the family, seeing if they're okay. I'm on special duty, you see. I have to make sure that the young princes are safe and well. Heirs to the throne and all that." She turns to her colleague and says, "You get off now – I'll wrap up here and sign us both out." With a nod he starts to walk on, briefly turning his head and calling out to us both, "Well, have a good one!"

"And are they?" I asked.

"Are they what?"

"Are they okay? The princes."

"Oh, yes. They're fine. Off on their way to Sandringham now." She looks wistful. "I wish I could be going there with them."

"You and I both. It's not ideal spending Christmas in a doorway," I laugh. She bends forward and leans towards me in a way that makes me want to sit up straight and pull my shoulders back. Smiling, she says in a low voice, almost a whisper, "Look, I'm my way home now. Why don't you come with me? It can't be much fun here on the street all on your own, Alexandra. And so cold. Brrr!" Even the way she shivers is elegant. "Come and get warm. Have a drink if you like."

"Really? You're most awfully kind, my dear. But is that allowed? I mean you're still in uniform, on duty."

"Oh, don't worry about that. I doubt that anyone will see me."

She sees the longing in my eyes. The hope of a warm house complete with glistening tree and log fire, a hot meal, and a soft bed. "Will there be crackers?" I ask, and then regret it as she lets out a hoot of laughter. Embarrassed, I look down. "Sorry. Sorry, I know that's stupid of me. I just used to really love pulling the
crackers when I was a child."

She leans down and gently puts a hand on my shoulder. "Oh, I'm not laughing at you Ally. It's just that we don't really go in for that kind of stuff where I come from. But if you want them, you can have them. You can have whatever you want. If you want crackers, there'll be crackers. If you want a tree, there'll be a tree. A roaring fire. Anything. Come on, follow me."

I stand up and clumsily attempt to scoop up my belongings; my handbag and a few plastic carriers, discarding the sleeping bag – that stays where it is. Wherever she takes me I will have to return, and I don't want to lose my doorway. Then it dawns on me, "Hey, how do you know my name?" I ask, but she's already stepping purposefully up the High Street, back towards the castle.

"Come on, leave that stuff there. You really don't need it where we're going," she calls over her shoulder. I drop the carrier bags and hurry after her. Still several paces ahead, she crosses the road, goes up Charlotte Street and into the castle grounds, with me following her like a little pet dog. Strangely the guards on duty don't stop us, or even seem to notice us. They just stand and stare ahead. It must be because they know her, I think.

It's a long time since I last came to the castle and I don't really recognise where I am, plus it's very dark out in the grounds now. I just follow her as she turns a corner into a narrow alleyway and stops abruptly outside an old oak door. She pushes it open and says, "Here we are, come on in." I enter a dark vestibule and struggle to see anything. Then she opens another interior door and I step inside. The first thing I notice is how warm it is; a log fire crackles in a huge stone fireplace. In spite of this, the room is quite compact and cosy. There's an inviting looking royal blue velvet sofa and a couple of armchairs – one in pink and one in green. In one corner of the room there is a beautiful, perfectly shaped Christmas tree complete with decorations and twinkling lights. I gasp. "Oh. This is gorgeous. Is this where you live?"

"I'm glad you like it. Sometimes I just hang out here. It's convenient for the work I do. Have a sit down and get properly warmed up. Now, how about a drink? What can I get you?"

Gratefully I sit on the pink armchair, leaning back and soaking up the smells of wood smoke and pine. Divine! "A brandy would be perfect. You're very kind…" I'm not sure what to call her. I always like to address people correctly, so I glance at her shoulder but can't really make out how many stripes there are, or even if there are any. I rub my eyes. Everything about her looks blurry. Apart from those eyes, which are as clear and blue as a summer sky. "Well, thank you and Merry Christmas, Ma'am, erm officer, erm, sergeant. Sorry, what shall I call you?"

She smiles, "Well, I've had a number of titles during my career and been called all kinds of things, but you can call me Rose."

"Well, Rose, rotten luck being on duty on Christmas Eve. But I guess there are worse assignments: you could be doing tomorrow. All those people that drink too much and start fighting. Families, eh? They're supposed to be your support, not your worst enemy. But you can't choose them."

Letting out a soft sigh and gently shaking her head as she hands me the brandy, Rose says, "Well, not usually, no. I did rather choose mine. But I think it was more a case of them choosing me. I'm afraid I was an awful disappointment to them." She sits down on the settee.

I chuckle. "Oh, my dear. I know how that feels. I was rather a disappointment to Mummy. I could have been here, you know - in the castle. I was a debutante. Oh, I know it was unofficial by then, but we still had the season, and I was quite a looker in my day. But I committed a terrible faux pas! Far worse than Fergie's toe sucking thing! But you're too young, you probably don't remember all that, do you?"

"Oh, I do. I knew her very well, actually."

"Really?" The brandy is taking effect; I feel warm and at ease.

"You seem a little, well..." I hesitate. "You know, well, a bit

classy for a police officer, if you don't mind me saying."

"Well, if you don't mind me saying, you seem awfully posh to be living in a sleeping bag in the street," she says. I laugh.

"It can happen to the best of us, you know. Prince Charles ran into an old school pal living on the streets a few years ago." She looks away, and then back at me. Now I'm in my flow – I don't often get the chance to chat to anyone and Rose seems happy to listen. "Between you and I, Rose, and I think you might find this hard to believe, but Mummy had Charles in her sights for me. And he wasn't uninterested. But then I drank a little too much one evening: well, honestly, I was completely trashed and did something regretful. And that was that. I was out of the running. Made way for Camilla and then Diana of course, poor dear. Like a lamb to the slaughter."

I looked up and was surprised to see her eyes brimming with tears. "Oh, my dear, are you okay? What's wrong? Have I said something?"

"No, Ally, you've brought back a few memories. We all do daft things sometimes, don't we?"

"Well, yes, we do. Look at me. How have I ended up in this sorry state? But we can't undo what we've done, can we? I just wish something would change and I could get my life back on track, but I think it's too late now. I'm old and there's nothing left for me." I sigh and shake my head, feeling deeply weary.

"Ally, you look so tired. Would you like to sleep now? You can stay here if you want."

"Oh, you are such a kind lady, Rose. I can't impose on you like this. Of course, I'd love to stay - forever, really. I'd like to go to sleep here and never wake up."

"You can do that too, if you really want. You have a choice. But think carefully. Life is for the living, Ally, and it's never too late until you're in your box. Then it really is over. It's Christmas Eve and that has always symbolised the start of a new, optimistic
age. A new beginning."

Feeling ever sleepier, I ask, "But how? How can I
change things?"

"Don't worry about that, Ally. The hardest part is deciding to change. The rest is easy. And there are lots of kind people out there who will help you. All you need to do is ask."

I've never felt so at peace; I feel my head drop and allow myself to drift off.

*****

When I wake up, the first thing I'm aware of is the cold. It's freezing! Confused, I open my eyes and see the hard grey pavement at my feet and above it the Round Tower. 'I knew it,' I think. 'That really would have been too good to be true. I was dreaming again.' As I pull my sleeping bag more tightly around me, I look up at the wintry sky. It's snowing! I can't help feeling a surge of childlike joy. "Merry Christmas!" I shout, to no one in particular.

"And Merry Christmas to you too! Here – let me give you some breakfast." A woman I've never seen before hands me a coffee and a croissant.

"God bless you," I say. This happens now and again; a kind soul who just wants to do something for us. She smiles, bends down and says, "Look, if you're interested, the church are doing Christmas dinner for anyone who has nowhere else to go. I'll come and get you and take you there if you like. It kicks off at eleven thirty with coffee and mince pies."

Now I know this sounds ungrateful, but I've always been proud. I've never wanted to rely on the charity of others. I even turned down a place in a homeless shelter once. I'm about to refuse when Rose's voice comes into my head. It's never too late to change, it seems to whisper. All you have to do is ask. So, I take a deep breath and say, "Well. Thank you. Yes, I would like that. I'd like that very much. Yes, please come and get me. I look forward to it."

She smiles and says, "I'm so glad. I'll see you shortly. Don't go anywhere!" Then off she goes. I sip my coffee, warming my hands around the cup. Time to freshen up. I rummage in my handbag for my wipes and my toothbrush (I do still have some pride, you know) when I feel something unfamiliar; it feels like a cardboard tube. Pulling it out, I'm truly surprised to see that it's a cracker! And a really lovely one at that – silver and sparkly with little pink and blue gems around the frills. "How on earth?" I ask out loud.

"Merry Christmas, Ally! You need someone to pull that with?" It's my neighbour, Fred, from the next doorway, standing in front of me wrapped in an old blanket, a can of Tennents already opened in one hand and his little black terrier sitting obediently at his feet. I stand up. "Good morning, Fred, and Merry Christmas to you."

"Glad to see you're okay this morning. I was a wee bit worried about you last night. You gave us a fright."

"I did? Why?"

"Well, when I walked past here last night, you didn't answer when I said goodnight."

"Oh. I don't remember. I must have fallen asleep early."

"Mmm. That was what was odd. It was really early. I should probably have checked. Maybe shaken you or something, but then the dog started whining and pulling at the lead, so I thought he needed to go for a shit. But I'm glad you're okay."

I hold out the cracker and he grabs the other end, laughing. As it bangs and breaks in two, out falls a paper crown and a small, shiny silver ring. I put it on my finger I see how pretty it looks, embellished with a tiny golden rose. I put on the paper crown.

"Well, won't you look at you, Ally," slurs Fred. "You look like a proper lady!" Laughing at the irony of this, I turn to look up the High Street. I glimpse a tall, blond, elegantly dressed woman. She smiles and waves at me. I blink and then she's gone.

Footnote 1

Goodbye England's Rose

Elton John re-wrote his song, "Candle in the Wind" which was about Marilyn Monroe. It was then dedicated to HRH Princess Diana and played at her funeral.

> *Goodbye England's rose*
> *May you ever grow in our hearts*
> *You were the grace that placed itself*
> *Where lives were torn apart...*

Footnote 2

"Fergie" was the nickname of Sarah Ferguson, who married Prince Andrew in 1986 to become the Duchess of York. She and Princess Diana were believed to be close friends, but in 1992 Fergie was photographed topless in the South of France with a lover. The incident was thereafter dubbed "the toe-sucking saga." Allegedly she blamed Diana for tipping off the press about her whereabouts and the two fell out, never to be reconciled. Fergie and Prince Andrew divorced in 1996.

5
Battleground Great Park
By Sue Blitz

Wherever there are trees, stories and mythologies have grown up around them. From the Greek fables of tree nymphs called dryads to Tolkein's Middle Earth's Ents. Throughout time there have been countless stories of individual trees that can come to life, or of magic forests that lure, entwine and trap innocent travellers or beautiful princesses.

Trees are symbols of growth, death, and rebirth. There are many rural communities who rely on forests for a livelihood, and this has, and does, build a powerful respect and reverence.

So, what business have these aeons of legend and superstition to do with Windsor, in the cyber-centric, fact-focused, pedantic 21st century?

Well may you ask. And the answer is best given by telling you a story that was told to me by a bearded stranger who crossed my path one late summer.

*****

I was sitting outside the Two Brewers, posting my photos of the Great Park on Instagram when a white-haired, bearded gentleman approached me. I thought he was going to ask to share the table. Instead, he remarked he had seen I had been taking pictures of the trees in the park and wanted to warn me about something.

Don't take Windsor Great Park at face value, he began. The lush, softly-rolling landscape with its confection of beautiful trees and docile creatures does its best to hide a place where once, not long ago, the natural world and the supernatural world vied for supremacy.

The trees of the Great Park, with their discarded flotsam and jetsam of fallen branches and long dead stumps, hold a steadfast claim to the landscape. They dig in and resolutely defy the hundreds of encounters that weave through their day.

They are witness to horse-riders drumming out a canter rhythm; walkers stepping lively; streaks of fluorescent yellow and pallid white freewheeling past; birds following their habitual trajectories through high canopies and low arbours; rabbits and hares lolloping languidly or bouncing buoyantly across meadows, and deer promenading in their nurseries, sororities or alone. In short, the visitors to the Great Park and its natural inhabitants are constantly on the move.

*****

For the trees, this movement and hubbub is the merest distraction. Their lives are built on a longer frame of time. Although every year they renew their garlands of blossoms and green cloaks, they often measure their lives not in months or years, but decades or centuries.

The oaks in particular brag amongst themselves who has lived the longest. They take a long view of life, which some joke is particularly fitting, as they grow within a country mile of the Long Walk.

Last year however, this equilibrium and serenity met a dramatic challenge. For as the seasons passed, as spring turned to summer and then autumn, these trees began to grow restless.

Perhaps it is because they were not as the trees of their youth, dwelling in the soft quiet of the deep, dark forest that Herne the Hunter knew so well. The trees were out of their element, finding themselves now living in a modern thoroughfare buzzing with hectic activity. For, whilst they learnt to know the animals and had developed a forbearance with their pace of life, the trees had begun to feel a jealousy towards the freedom of movement that the human beings were blatantly enjoying.

The trees were out of sorts, their mounting resentment of the animal kingdom made them thoroughly unsettled, from their roots to their bark. And as the autumn days of that year progressed, the poison of this envy grew within them. Whether they were oak, elm, birch, beech or horse chestnut, the trees knew they had to do something to calm this vile covetousness that was damaging their very nature. Then gradually, between them, they devised a way to satiate the green-eyed monster within.

*****

The bearded stranger paused his tale and glanced at me and my empty pint glass. I sighed, went to the bar, and ordered us both a pint of bitter. I placed it in front of him and he continued.

Do you understand what was happening? The trees had become jealous of those living in a quicker time frame, the ambulant who cross whole fields in a matter of minutes rather than cover patches of land in several years. They yearned to move at a quicker pace, they tortured themselves with this desire, but it seemed irksomely impossible. That was until one of the old wise oaks glanced down to the ground and saw what was hidden in plain sight.

You've probably seen what he saw then and dismissed them as constructs of your vivid imagination. The broken old trunks and branches that resemble all kinds of animals and creatures. There's a branch in Queen Anne's Ride that is honey-toned and smooth to the touch; it looks from a distance like a preening deer. Not far from Bear Rails there lurks a velociraptor. A bough that bends towards the path, as a raptor would towards its prey. Then there's the Giant Octopus in a path adjacent to the Long Walk, the quasi-creature crawls along the field as its fellow cephalopods do along the seabed. And of course, there's The Ogre, its pained expression glaring out from the trunk of the tree.

The tree spirit within the wise oak stirred and remembered the old times when deals could be forged with the supernatural forces of nature. She knew that it would need all the spirits within the trees to muster together a huge strength of will. With sufficient determination they could summon up magical forces that would help them possess these semblances of creatures. These creatures would be the key to giving them the gift of rapid movement they so dreadfully desired.

Where could they find such tremendous power? It would have to be conjured from a very magical source. Traditionally mystic events that could provide such forces, such as the Summer Solstice and All Hallows Eve had come and gone. What was left for the year to offer? Ah yes, of course, the powerful magic that is created on Christmas Eve.

*****

And then it was Christmas Eve. The night was still and cold, with a luminous moon obscured from time to time by veils of cloud. When the moon was shining, the trees cast ominous shadows that shed an even deeper pall of darkness onto the ground.

Doubtless there would be a frost before dawn broke.

All around Windsor town, church bells began to strike out the midnight hour. As the first chime cut through the crisp night air, the sound waves travelled to the Great Park and hit a tree. The tree reverberated and thrilled to the vibration's blow and passed the impulse of sound onto the next tree, who passed it on to its nearest neighbours. The second chime followed close behind and it echoed throughout the park, with all the trees and their spirits hungrily lapping up the sound waves. By the time the third chime struck, every single tree had greedily consumed any noise the night air had served.

As the trees had rightly worked out, the Christmas Eve chimes were magical enough to power-up the spirits that always have lived and always will live. Once woken, the tree spirits got to work. They began to possess any discarded branches, dead trunks or living trees that resembled animals.

A beautiful caramel-coloured, preening deer finished grooming itself and stood, at first shakily, upon its four legs. A prehistoric velociraptor yawned and sniffed the night air; there was much sprinting and pouncing to look forward to. A giant octopus flexed and relaxed, propelling itself through the grass with the speed and elegance that satisfied all who saw her.

One of the oddest consequences of all this supernatural movement in the Great Park was the effect it had on the passing of time. Whilst all around was moving at a rapid pace, time itself had decided to slow down. Hence even before the fourth chime of midnight struck, the changeling trees had established themselves as action-packed creatures. They gained confidence in their ability to move, they raced and roistered over the fields, which they had only looked at from afar. There was a joy in exploring what was around the next corner, a glorious indulgence in snuffling around the ponds and marshy areas they had never even glimpsed before.

For the tree-creatures, it seemed a week had passed when the seventh chime struck. After all their hyperactivity, it will be no surprise to hear that they were beginning to feel a little tired and perhaps a bit tetchy. Their emotions were beginning to get out of control, the jealousy they felt towards other species was starting to turn back on themselves.

One by one they began to dwell on envious thoughts. How come that tree-creature over there can leap higher, or that one over there can run faster than me? They don't deserve that freedom. I do. And yes, there is something rather cunning and rather nasty that can be done about it.

The temperature in the Great Park dropped a degree or so. The moon clouded over, and an icy wind began to stir. A deer-shaped tree looked over its shoulder. Was that a lioness stalking him? Was that fear he was feeling?

The angry ogre felt the anger within him mount. He felt nothing but hate towards the lithe and beautiful octopus; he could catch the beast with his long branch claws and stop it in its tracks. And now the ogre would show the octopus who was superior.

A fury possessed all of them like nothing they had experienced before. It felt like a great storm, when the dark clouds, piercing rain, terrifying winds and thunder and lightning rampaged through the park. Certainly frightening, but strangely thrilling. Nature coming into its own, establishing her presence on a world that often forgot it was she who was in charge.

The feeling rose and rose, a tornado of vitriol that nothing could abate. This episode of wild rage came to an end when the twelfth chime of midnight rang out.

The sound of the last of the Christmas Eve peals cut through the battleground, severing the power of the tree spirits, and soothing the ire of the trees. Leaving the park bathed in a strange stillness and serenity.

*****

I thought the man had finished his story, but he pointed to my phone and then, recalling shots I had uploaded of the weird-shaped trunks and trees of the Great Park, he spoke softly, in a voice that I strained to hear. Don't expect to see the transmogrified creatures in exactly the same place that you've heard me describe. In fact, don't even expect to see them in the last place you saw them.

I glanced at the trees on my phone again, and then back at the storyteller. But he had gone, melting into the stream of tourists making their way through the gates onto the Long Walk. Strangely enough for such a close encounter, I can barely remember what the white-haired gentleman looked like, but what I do remember is the comforting smell of warm cinnamon and cloves that wafted about him.

6
Mamie
By Amanda Buchan

I was returning from work to Mamie's. I had cleaned up after five Windsor office parties, crushed paper hats into the rubbish, washed glasses and coaxed the publicity manager out of the toilet and into the street just before she was sick. That bit of the day was completed, and it was then, as I hurried through the cold rain and the festive lights, that I was quite suddenly overwhelmed with the excitement of a family Christmas.

Christmas was never celebrated much in my home, in my childhood, but in another childhood in my imagination, it would have been as colourful and sentimental as a Victorian illustration. Windsor gave me my first real Christmas.

The town has an advent calendar setting with the castle a theatrical backdrop to the bustling town below. There are proper decorations and shop windows and carol singers and a public Christmas tree. The royal family never appears at this time of year, but the invisible existence of a Queen with a crown adds to the atmosphere of celebration.

We all lived with Mamie. I hadn't meant to live with Mamie, none of us had, but soon none of us wanted to live anywhere else. Mamie owned a big, dark Victorian house with turrets and bay windows. She had lived there alone for years, and then she was burgled. They broke in downstairs and although they hardly stole anything because Mamie kept her jewellery in a hot water bottle, she began to feel lonely and unsafe, and she offered Felix a room in exchange for companionship and burglar prevention. No one could possibly imagine Felix stopping a burglar, but he might delay one by discussing religion until the police came. Felix is an enthusiastic believer. When I met him, he ran a charity shop in Peascod Street - he still does - and he calls the numbers at bingo twice a week. Mamie loved bingo from the moment she discovered it.

The other person in the house was Joe, a Scot who works in a key cutting, shoe mending place. Joe was in prison for GBH, so he would really have been better than Felix with burglars.

We were an eccentric foursome, all fugitives from our different pasts, and we became a family.

Mamie, Felix, and Joe had far more interesting pasts than I, who had lived all my life in the greyest part of a grey town. My father appeared and disappeared from time to time but I didn't need him, and he showed no sign of needing me. Perhaps he wasn't my father. My mother was a dusty little person, frightened of my father, devoted to my father, constantly anxious about my father and occasionally about me.

When it was just the two of us, my mother used to take me to the library; it became my second home. I read everything I could. I loved my English teacher. She said I lived in my imagination, and she was right. I dreamed of magic, romance, music, and colour until they were more real than the monotony that surrounded me.

Then my father returned permanently, bringing with him a younger half-sister I didn't know I had, and my home suddenly was not my home. My books, my belongings and especially I myself were in the way.

A school friend's aunt lived in Windsor. I would have preferred some faraway land, but it sounded distant enough to be an escape, even an adventure. It was agreed I could stay for a while in exchange for babysitting.

The first Christmas away did not feel much like an adventure. I missed my sad little mother and I called her. She wanted me back, but my father was still there, so I gave up what had been my home.

My welcome as a babysitter wore thin and I got a job cleaning offices, but I earned very little. I met Felix when I was trying on a coat in the charity shop. He said, "You can't possibly wear that, you look like a llama." I did. We spent an hour laughing and choosing clothes, and I never paid for them. I think Felix must have. I asked him whether he knew anyone with a cheap room. A few days later he suggested I come to Mamie's, and my life changed.

I am still not sure why Mamie agreed to have us all in her house, but she must have liked us. She used to say, "Everyone needs to be needed" and it was true. I had never felt needed, but she made us all feel not just needed but valued, amusing, important and part of the family.

Mamie had the top floor including a little room she called her boudoir. Joe, who had been there almost a year, had a room on the first floor, and I had one at the back overlooking the garden. It still had an alphabet frieze round the wall. I could watch the birds and squirrels and see the sun set behind the trees, and I imagined the child who used to live there, doing the same before she went to bed.

Mamie was half-French; she still had an accent. Her family had lived in a chateau, and they had paintings, porcelain and embroidered linen and a huge cat called Melchior. When her parents died, she sold the chateau and moved to Paris with Melchior. He was a white Persian and she loved him even more than the English Army officer whom she married and moved with to Windsor. When Melchior died and her husband was killed in Ireland, she mourned them both, alone in the big Windsor house, until the robbery.

Felix's room was on the ground floor, to be on hand for burglars.

He had a car called The Rhino; it was grey and very old but strangely reliable. Someone from Leeds had lent it to him permanently. The Rhino took us on summer picnics and winter excursions. Felix was at the centre of a huge support network, stretching across the country, a mafia of workers in charity shops. If you needed something, or some information, he could find it through his contacts in almost any village or town, sometimes even beyond Britain. The smartest charity shops in Europe were in Brussels he said, especially at Christmas; he had on occasion found treasures there when he needed treasure. He played a sort of Robin Hood, persuading rich people to give him valuable objects, which he usually sold through dealers, and designer clothes, which he sold in his or other charity shops. He must have made a fortune for the charity. Nobody seemed to regulate him, and he never had any money of his own.

I sometimes sat drinking tea with Mamie while she told me stories about soirées in Paris, how the city suffered in the war, about her life as an officer's wife. I told her about my mother, and she put her arm around me, and to my surprise that made me cry. She talked politics and religion with Felix and food with Joe, and she reminisced about Melchior to all of us. She and Felix debated about whether cats have souls. Mamie believed absolutely that they do, so did Joe, Felix wasn't sure. I didn't see why they shouldn't.

We always had afternoon tea together when we got back from work. Mamie presided. She had a porcelain teapot, with a pattern of birds and flowers, matching cups and a pretty milk jug and there was always cake.

Mamie was older than she pretended. She always looked elegant and when she went to bingo with her hair swept up in what she called a chignon; she only looked about 60 but she must have been at least 75.

She received two pensions, which paid for running the house, but not for food, especially the amount Joe and Felix ate, so we all contributed. Mamie didn't cook much except cakes; she was very good at cakes, so Joe and I cooked everything else. Joe taught me how to cook. I wondered at first whether he had learnt in prison, but his dishes and sauces were never learnt in a prison kitchen; he had worked in a restaurant and it was the head cook he had grievously bodily harmed.

Joe and I made plans for Christmas dinner. Joe was as excited as a child. It was his first Christmas after prison, and he wanted to give everyone treats. We worked out how much all the ingredients would be and then we went to see Mamie. She already had plans for Christmas but not for cooking, except that she was making a Christmas cake. She had money for a turkey and all the things we had listed but insisted on an apricot soufflé as she said English Christmas Pudding was too heavy.

I arrived back from cleaning that evening the day before Christmas Eve, looking forward to a cup of tea and wondering when Mamie would produce the Christmas cake. I had cold fingers and ears and damp feet, and I was tired. I came through the door and the house was transformed into something from my childhood dreams. The hall was lit with candlelight, and I could see as I went towards the sitting room more candles, white and gold, a tree decorated with stars and golden birds and the fireplace alive with flaming logs. A spicy scent rose from a silver incense burner. Mamie was already drinking afternoon tea. She was wearing long sparkling earrings: she had a large collection of earrings from plastic hoops to a beautiful pair of gold and ruby teardrops. "You look frozen, we are having Russian vanilla tea. As soon as the boys are home, we will have the Christmas cake. I serve it always before Christmas. On Christmas Day nobody wants cake, not even Joe."

Before I met Mamie, I didn't know there was such a thing as Russian tea, and I had never smelled frankincense, nor had my senses and my imagination ever been so stimulated. Mamie's house was full of books, she taught me and Joe to play chess as she said she was tired of beating Felix and we all went to bingo. "Unfortunate happenings can lead to unexpected blessings," she often said. Windsor and the charity shop were certainly that for me; perhaps we were all unexpected blessings for Mamie. In a matter-of-fact but magical fashion with her porcelain teacups, her earrings, and her bingo, she changed my life, and I became myself.

Then it was presents. I had bought a cologne I knew Joe liked and I had knitted Felix a scarf from wool that was left in the charity shop as I knew he would be pleased I had made it myself, but Mamie: what could we give her? Nothing was enough or right, and then I had an idea. I shared it with Felix and Joe. It was risky, but we all agreed it was a risk worthy of Mamie.

On Christmas Eve, Felix, Joe, and I went in The Rhino to the Dog and Cat Rescue Centre near Old Windsor to collect Mamie's Christmas present. Felix and I had already been there, and we had seen him; the cat worthy of Mamie. He stood apart from the others, a small dark cat with tufted ears like a little lynx. When we came to the cage, he stretched and picked his way to the door, stepped into the basket we had brought without a backward turn and as we drove home, he stared straight ahead.

"Keep him in your room," said Felix, "We are going to Midnight Mass tonight so we will present him to her after breakfast in the morning."

"Midnight Mass?"

"Mamie and I always go to Midnight Mass in St George's Chapel on Christmas Eve."

"Isn't it just for the royal family?"

"Of course not, you can come if you like."

So, on a cold, drizzly Christmas Eve, Joe and I followed Felix and Mamie up the hill to the castle. We joined the queue of people filing through the huge gateway, past the sentry boxes, across the parade ground the lawn and up to the exquisite chapel. It was already nearly full inside, but the size and height

73

and the soaring roof made it seem spacious. There were service sheets with the words of the carols. Felix is a believer, but he used to surprise me sometimes with his views: "I hope they don't have 'The First Nowell', such a boring carol, and ridiculous words," but he knew every word of every carol by heart.

I sat between him and Joe, who had never been to the chapel either. I was fascinated by the choir, half of them men, and half boys, and some so young they could hardly be seen over the heads of the people in front of me.

A young boy began to sing, unaccompanied by music, alone in that vast expanse of the ancient space with hundreds and hundreds of people listening. The voice was effortless, climbing to high, high notes, hardly a human voice. I found my throat was hurting and tears were streaming down my face. I glanced at Felix, he caught my eye and smiled, as though crying in a carol service was what you should do. Then we sang 'In the Bleak Midwinter' and the poet's words spoke of hope and a safe haven from the cold, and I felt it was my carol.

We all thronged out, past the huge figures of the Christmas crib, the angel and the donkey, the splendid genuflecting kings and Mary with her carved secret face, and into the cold reality of the night. 'Happy Christmas,' 'Merry Christmas,' everyone was greeting each other, people I had never seen.

"I don't count it as a real Christmas till Christmas breakfast time," announced Mamie.

We went home and had bedtime hot chocolate and brandy before turning in for the night.

"What about you know who?" I whispered to Felix.

"Give him some milk and bring him down at present time."

Mamie had been up for an hour, preparing coffee and the special Christmas cinnamon buns that she always made. Presents were after breakfast. When Felix asked me to get Mamie's present, I was afraid she might not want him. He perched alert in my arms, and I handed him to her. She placed him on her lap, and they looked at each other without saying anything, then the cat yawned, and Mamie looked up and smiled a huge smile.

"I have taken the liberty of naming him Casper," said Felix.

She laughed, "You knew I would call him Casper."

My present was a train ticket to my old town and money to stay a night in a hotel. "Just in case you want to visit her," said Mamie. Felix gave me a fluffy black wool coat, from a very superior charity shop in Holland Park. Joe gave me a key ring with a llama on it and a book of Highland recipes.

Casper slept until dinner, when he created havoc with wrapping paper and apricot soufflé.

All this was eight years ago. Felix and Joe and I still live in Mamie's house. She left it to us, but we still think of it as hers. Casper died a few days after she did. We maintain Mamie's Christmas traditions, the candles and the tree and Midnight Mass, and Joe makes a Christmas cake, which we still eat before Christmas. We need each other and for now we are happy with that.

Last Christmas Felix and Joe brought me a fluffy grey kitten. "He looks like a llama," said Felix, "His name is Balthazar."

Tea with Father Christmas
By Amanda Buchan

I was going to be an architect: he an actor, we knew we were the first ever to experience real love.

Our daughter was two when he went. He sends postcards and beautiful unexpected presents and erratically, money. Sometimes he calls.

Occasionally, with a lurch I see him on television: a gang member, a waiter, a courtier.

She is five now. We went to Daniel's to see Father Christmas.

I knew at once it was him, even through the silly beard, that smile.

We three had tea afterwards. She was ecstatic: tea with Father Christmas!

7
A Christmas in Time
By Rosa Carr

Like clockwork each year, on the 1st of November, the shops took down their Halloween decorations and put up the Christmas ones.

Thankfully, the town centres don't put up their lights and decorations until a bit later in the month, she thought.

Alice walked briskly back home after work. She had left early today, and it was still light out. Walking past a homeless man bundled in layers of clothing; she felt around in her jacket pocket for spare change. She walked another few hundred metres and saw a woman sitting there, but she had no more coins and felt a pang of guilt for this woman. Alice reached up and pulled off her scarf and handed it to her.

"Bless you, thank you!"

As she continued walking, she overheard a man talking on his phone, "I know I haven't seen you in a year Mum, but I think I'm going to stay here for the holidays... Yes, there may be a girl involved, someone I knew at uni... You don't know her... Her name is Ella..." The man turned down Peascod Street, and Alice smiled for the happy couple. She felt a slight pang at not being able to see her parents this year either — but someone had to cover the office this year, and it had fallen to her.

Along her route there was an alleyway that would cut out part of her journey. Looking at the sky, she judged that it was still early enough to take this route safely. The alley led to a little courtyard which Alice crossed, and halfway along, a flickering light caught her attention out of the corner of her eye. She halted and turned in that direction.

She searched for the source but didn't see anything. She had turned her head a fraction to continue when the light sparked back into life.

It came from an archway leading off the alleyway.

How strange! I don't remember ever seeing that before! she thought as she diverted off her homeward path. There was no one around. Her caution lost out to her curiosity.

She walked through the archway and found herself in a vestibule, which had arches and doorways around the circular enclosure.

Alice peered around the nearest arch and saw a utility room with tools and sandbags pushed up along the walls.

Moving to the door next to this room, Alice could just see through the little window in the middle: a grass path leading to a dormant garden covered in snow. Snow? Alice frowned. There hasn't been any snow yet. Someone had obviously gone all out to decorate for Christmas. She tried the handle and found it unyielding.

Shrugging, she moved on to the next arch, which looked as though it came out at the other end of her short-cut. She paused for a moment, debating whether to continue on her way home.

Curiouser and curiouser! I hope I don't end up like the proverbial cat!

The next door also had a window, but this one was at a more accessible height for Alice. She looked through and saw a cobbled road that she didn't recognise. She tried the door handle, which gave way. Pulling open the door, she stepped over the threshold. The door swung shut behind her. With the click of the door, she left the modern world behind and felt a weight pulling at her body.

Alice looked down: where seconds before had been jeans tucked into boots and her thick padded waterproof jacket, now sat the weight of a structured velvet dress, cape, and high-heeled shoes.

She looked around: she was still on the High Street, up there was the church, and she could see the castle. But…

Alice did a double take.

There were horses which weren't an uncommon sight in Windsor. A horse attached to a carriage — again, this was also common enough for the tourists.

But! Alice couldn't quite grasp the concept in her logical mind.

There wasn't only one horse and carriage. There were many. That's all she could see around her, and no cars!

Alice looked at her clothes again and then at the carriages. She was…

"Mistress! What are you doing?" A girl, not much younger than Alice, asked as she approached.

"I…" Alice couldn't finish the sentence. What was she doing? "I don't know."

"Well, you best not keep Sir Henry waiting," the girl said, trying to usher Alice forward.

"I don't…" Alice trailed off again.

"Miss, have you taken ill?"

"No, no ... I just…"

Before Alice could come up with an excuse, a tall man strode up the road towards them. The girl curtsied and edged behind Alice.

"Ah, Miss Adelaide, there you are. Elizabeth and I became concerned. My dear sister is having hysterics in the tea-room. Shall we?" he asked, holding out his arm. Alice was helpless to refuse and looped her arm through his.

Alice allowed herself to be guided along the road, which she noticed had no tar, but instead was cobbled and covered in sand and straw. She saw that the Parish Church was where it should be. But opposite it was not a restaurant but a photography studio. And there was the Guildhall, but out in the Cornmarket, was — well, it was an actual market, selling grain. And opposite — Alice

turned to look — was not the bank but a drapery.

Alice paused her tennis-match-like spectatorship of the shops, as her companion guided her up alongside the Guildhall and towards a tea-room that they entered.

As she was led to a table, a young lady, maybe a bit younger than Alice, stood up.

"Oh Henry, you found her. Adelaide, I was ever so worried! What happened to you?"

"I...um … I got distracted," Alice said, as she sat down.

Adelaide? As in Queen Adelaide? The wife of King William IV, who ruled before Queen Victoria. Alice had seen the name around town often enough — in fact, she lived not too far from the Royal Adelaide Hotel. She was not being treated as a royal, which meant that she – whoever she was impersonating – must be named after that queen?

So, if I was named after Queen Adelaide - wait, I'm not Adelaide, I'm Alice. What is going on?! Am I… is this in the past? Did I time travel to Victorian times?

"Oh dear, no doubt you saw a fine dress at the dress-makers' shop?"

"Yes, Elizabeth, you are right, I did find Miss Adelaide near the dressmakers."

Alice smiled weakly. She looked around the room and saw other well-dressed groups having afternoon tea. She couldn't see her — maid? — the girl she was with when she stepped out of the courtyard.

The courtyard! I need to get back there.

She sat through the tea and nodded politely at the conversation.

"Care for a stroll through the park, Miss Adelaide?" Henry asked, as they made their way out of the tea-room.

"Oh Henry, I must stop at the dressmakers and pick up my shawl for tomorrow night. You know that the theatre gets draughty in winter."

Henry looked torn between his sister and Adelaide.

"Henry, you go with Adelaide and her maid can chaperone," Elizabeth said, as the girl appeared. "I will go with my maid, Dorothy." Another girl stood nearby.

Chaperone? Alice thought. Who is this man?

When Henry hesitated a moment longer, Elizabeth gave him a gentle shove towards Adelaide. He held out his arm again, and with some encouragement from Elizabeth, Alice placed her hand on his arm.

She tried to angle them towards the courtyard, but Henry firmly steered her towards a carriage. He helped her in and then followed. She saw the maid being helped up next to the driver. I need to find out her name!

"Are you looking forward to the theatre tomorrow?"

"Oh… yes, absolutely." Alice said, feigning interest as she hoped that she would wake up from this dream before then.

Alice sat awkwardly opposite Henry. He was good-looking enough with his sandy-brown hair and blue eyes. While he was the perfect gentleman, Alice felt an undercurrent of something that she couldn't quite place. He is different to any man I've ever dated.

After the five-minute trundle down the road, the carriage stopped near the Long Walk. Henry stepped out and held his hand out for Alice.

When she had followed him out, she tried to pull her hand back; but instead, he held on to it and looped her arm around his elbow, towing her along.

That's what's different! It's the possessive way that men treated women in this time.

As they walked down the Long Walk, Alice marvelled at the lack of twenty-first-century security: there were no bollards to ruin the view.

Henry was talking about Christmas as Alice tuned in again. "… and of course, we will attend the service with your family."

"Yes," Alice said, trying to affect meekness. *Service? He doesn't mean church service, does he?* Alice hadn't attended a church since her grandparents wanted her to participate as a child.

How far away was Christmas? Please let me be gone by then.

Henry directed them back up the path, even though they had only been walking for ten minutes. As they turned, she saw the maid waiting for them to walk past before trailing behind them again.

They all got into the carriage for the five-minute ride down the road back to the High Street. They alighted past the Guildhall near Peascod Street. Alice stretched up to look down the street. *Where is Starbucks? M&S? Those random shops selling mobile phone covers? This confirms my earlier deduction.* Instead of bunting and fairy lights outside each shop, there was meat and poultry displayed.

"Miss," a timid voice murmured at her shoulder. "The carriage."

"Thank you," Alice said, as Henry helped her into her own carriage.

"Up you come, Grace," said the gruff voice of the driver.

Grace! Her name is Grace.

*****

She had woken up, disappointed to still be in Victorian times. She had gone to sleep eagerly wishing that she would wake up in her own warm, insulated room, under a feather duvet, instead of in a draughty room with only the embers of a fire and a brazier under her mattress.

Alice was thankful to have Grace around. The girl didn't seem to notice that Alice had no idea what to do. Grace simply went about dressing Alice, and then guided her downstairs to the dining room.

Alice sat down at the table, which was spread out with a plateful of breakfast foods. Presumably that was Adelaide's father at the head of the table reading the newspaper, and opposite Alice guessed that the other man must be a brother?

The older man put down his newspaper at Alice's shoulder and turned to the younger man. "Have you heard about what…" Alice tuned out and looked at the newspaper.

23 December 1879.

She scanned the page, but something caught her attention:

Prominent barrister, Richard Pankhurst marries Emmeline Goulden, at St Luke's Church, Pendleton on 18 December 1879.

Emmeline Pankhurst!

"Goodbye, Adelaide."

Alice looked up as the men left the room.

She pulled out the page with the announcements and then headed up to her room.

*****

"Miss, don't forget your cape. It's frosty today."

"Thank you, Grace," Alice said, stepping out of the house as she fastened her cape. She was accompanying Adelaide's mother to the dressmaker to pick up her dress for the theatre tonight. They spent about thirty minutes at the dressmakers while the older woman had a final fitting for the dress.

"Thank you. Come along, dear, let us get back."

84

They were standing outside the shop when a boy darted past them. "Wells, be back in five minutes, or you will get a flogging," He turned away from the boy and bobbed his head at Adelaide's mother, "Oh, my apologies, madam." The man stepped back inside the drapery shop as the boy ran down the street.

Their carriage had stopped in front of them as Alice saw the young boy hurtling down the street, clutching a parcel. Nearing the carriage, he bumped into someone in his haste and dropped his package.

In slow motion, Alice saw the horse spook and rear up, legs flying. Without a thought, Alice reached forward and grabbed the boy's jacket just as the horse's massive hooves clattered back down on the street.

Alice pulled the boy close for a moment and then held him at arm's length. His eyes were as wide as saucers, but he looked unharmed.

"Miss!"

"Adelaide!"

"Wells!"

The shouting came from all directions, but Alice focused on the boy.

"What's your name?"

"H-Herbert," he whispered. "Herbert Wells."

"Are you hurt?"

"No, Miss."

The man from the drapery shop grabbed the boy roughly. "Are you harmed? Is the fabric damaged?"

"Calm down, he is fine, just had a shock," Alice intervened, "And your parcel is surely not worth the life of a boy?"

The man glared at Alice for a moment, taking in her fine clothing and his eyes swept to the carriage behind. He forced the corners of his mouth up, as he released the boy, and bobbed his head forward. "Of course, Miss, you are quite right. Thank you for your kindness."

The carriage driver stepped forward for a word with the man.

Alice leaned against the wall for a moment. "I know that H.G. Wells spent some time in Windsor as a boy. Did I just time-travel to save H.G. Wells?" she whispered to herself.

She looked around and saw that the boy was standing nearby looking at her with wide eyes. The draper and the driver had finished their discussion.

"Adelaide, get in here," called the older woman.

Alice got in and was immediately greeted with a barrage of hysterics. She tuned out, but occasionally the words 'you could have been killed' or 'highly improper' and 'not ladylike' interrupted her thoughts.

H.G. Wells! I have just met the young H.G. Wells. I'm actually sitting in a Victorian carriage having met one of the forefathers of sci-fi literature. Oh! Could I have inspired his work? Wow!

This brush with someone who would be famous, had put her in such high spirits that she coasted along through the rest of the day without noticing much. Later that evening, she even greeted Henry warmly and saw him beaming in return. Over dinner before the theatre, Alice listened politely as the group heard about her outlandish heroics earlier that day.

"You should have seen her; no consideration for my constitution. She grabbed that urchin with no thought."

"Ah, but Lady Moore, I believe the child was not an urchin, but in the employ of Rodgers and Denyer."

But the older woman just waved her hand at Henry and continued her hysterical account.

When the story ended, Henry said, "While highly irresponsible to put your life at risk for a common child, I am glad that you are unharmed and showed such courage in saving his poor life. To Miss Adelaide!"

Despite the backhanded compliment, Alice felt as bubbly as the champagne being toasted in her honour.

Later, she rather enjoyed herself at the theatre, sitting in the luxury of the box seats with Henry. From the little attention she had paid to the performance, it seemed enjoyable.

*****

The next day was Christmas Eve. Grace told her that morning as she helped Alice dress, that Cook had been up since four in the
morning preparing the feast for that evening and tomorrow.

It turned out that Grace wasn't as timid as Alice's first impression had suggested.

Alice guessed that Grace was around sixteen years old. She had a confidence and charisma that was unusual in this period, as Alice believed that women were treated as inferior.

"Grace?"

"Yes, miss?"

Alice hesitated. She didn't want to overstep and change history, but she felt deep down that Grace had a much brighter future than being an ordinary maid in a grand house.

"I want to show you something."

"All right, miss?"

Alice pulled out the newspaper page. "If you can, I want you to try to seek employment with this lady."

"Why miss? Who is she?"

"She is someone that I've heard of, and I... think that she will do great things."

"Great things? What do you mean?"

"She's influential, and I think she will do great things for society. Here, I'll write you a reference, should you need it."

Alice went to the small writing desk and pulled out some paper, a pen, and opened an ink well. She tried to write as neatly and as elegantly as her twenty-first-century scrawl would allow. Alice handed the letter along with the newspaper page to Grace.

"Thank you, miss. I don't know if I'll ever leave, but I thank you for this. Now we had better finish getting you ready."

*****

After a grand feast, joined by Henry, Elizabeth, and their family, the two families made their way to church.

Alice hadn't been to church since she was a child. Her parents weren't religious, and although both sets of grandparents had tried to teach Alice about religion, she, like her parents, had no interest.

It was a spectacular sight, however, entering a Victorian church. It was a beautiful structure with a vast ceiling, and even in the dim candlelight, the stained-glass windows sparkled their rainbow colours over the smartly dressed congregation.

Alice tried to pay attention to the sermon but found that her mind drifted off occasionally.

Will I be stuck here forever? What about the real Adelaide?

I must try and find a way to the alleyway again.

She followed the actions of her companions, and eventually, they left the church and got into carriages back to their houses.

*****

On Christmas Day, Grace helped dress Alice again.

Alice used to think that the rich were too lazy to dress themselves, but it turned out that there was a lot more to it than the modern shirt and trousers. There were a few layers of undergarments, then the corset, and the crinoline.

Alice held onto the post of her bed as Grace yanked on the strings imprisoning her chest and limiting her breath.

"Miss, do you know what happened to your shawl?"

"My shawl?"

"Yes, the one you wore last night to church."

"Oh… uh…" Alice thought back. She had felt a bit hot in the church despite the freezing temperatures outside. "Did you check the carriage?"

"Yes, miss. It was not there."

"I suppose it must be in the church. Shall we go?"

Grace hesitated. "I suppose they can spare me for an hour. I'll ask for the carriage."

The carriage neared the High Street.

"Oh!" Alice called out as they passed the alleyway.

"What's wrong, miss?"

"Tell the driver to stop."

Grace called out to the driver, who halted the horses.

"What is it, miss?"

Alice wasn't listening. She got out and walked towards the alleyway.

"Miss! What are you doing?"

That snapped Alice out of her daze. She turned to look at Grace.

"Promise me, Grace. Promise that you will find Mrs Pankhurst and help her."

"Yes, miss. I will."

"Even if I don't seem to remember this or know what you're talking about."

Grace frowned.

"Promise!"

"Yes, yes, I promise I will."

"Please wait here," Alice said, walking down the alley.

There was the courtyard. She hesitated and then went inside. There were the doors. She recognised the one she had used before. She gripped the handle, then looked back.

"This isn't my time," she whispered, and pulled the door open.

Author's Note

A big thank you to Louisa and Barbara from the Windsor Museum for their help on this.

It is a fact that H.G. Wells worked in Windsor as a child.

Book references: Windsor in Victorian Times by Angus Macnaghten (1975)

8
Labyrinthitis
by June Kerr

"Labyrinthitis," the Doctor stated matter-of-factly.

I'd never heard of it. It sounded like a children's fantasy film or a game show like The Crystal Maze or something, but it turned out I had a really bad infection in my middle ear, which explained the dizzy feeling and the many falls.

A month later, I was still feeling dizzy, but at least the medication had stopped the frequency of the falling. Mark had been amazing, even though we'd officially split up, he was still very much part of my life and had called me every day during my illness to see how I was doing. He'd even popped round a couple of times and offered his sexual services; had I been feeling better, I might have taken him up on the offer, but it turns out labyrinthitis makes you feel like total crap.

Christmas was fast approaching and, as my family were up North and I still wasn't feeling up to flying, I had arranged to spend it with Sue, one of my best friends who lived about an hour's drive from home in Windsor. Arriving around 6pm on Christmas Eve, there was barely time for a quick 'Hello' before I was ushered out and into the local pub for the first drink I'd had in almost 6 weeks. An hour later I was done, convincing Sue that it was just too much too soon and all I needed was an hour's shut-eye and I'd be right as rain again. I took her keys and lay myself down in the spare room, promising I'd be back by 9pm and ready to party.

I woke just after 11pm feeling dreadful. All I wanted to do was go home and get into my own bed. So, I packed myself into my car, left Sue a note wishing her Merry Christmas and that I would call her the next day to explain, drove the hour back home to Windsor, got under my duvet and woke up at 7am on Christmas morning alone, dizzy and totally miserable. I'd never spent Christmas on my own. I had no food, no plans to see friends, no presents to open and I felt so dizzy that I couldn't even stand up without feeling that I was going to pass out.

Mark phoned.

"Merry Christmas babe, how's it going at Sue's?"

I explained tearfully where I was and why and without hesitation, he told me he would pick me up at 12.30 as he was taking me round to his mum's to join the family for Christmas lunch.

"I can't, Mark. Firstly, I've not been invited and secondly, I don't have any more of the anti-dizziness tablets as I finished the course and thought I was over it."

"Can you get any?"

"Well, I could try I suppose."

And I did. I called the emergency on-call doctor and explained the situation. He arranged for a prescription to be sent to the pharmacy that was open in Windsor. I dragged myself out of bed, showered and dressed and shakily walked the few minutes from my house to Peascod Street to pick it up.

It felt cold and crisp outdoors, with a hint of frost in the air and a smattering of ice in the corners of some of the shop windows and doorways. The Christmas lights that were strung across Peascod Street were glowing blurs of reds, blues, and greens in the bracing air, resplendent against the backdrop of Windsor Castle, which sat at the top of the street on the hill. It looked and felt so 'Christmassy' that I could feel my mood beginning to brighten. I made my way to the chemist, peering in the shop windows at their artful displays of Christmas goodies set amongst their lights and decorations and wondering if the

Royal Family were at Windsor Castle for Christmas this year or at Balmoral as normal.

"Can you spare any change, love?" a disembodied voice asked from under a crumpled bundle of coats and blankets in a shop doorway.

"Sorry. I didn't see you there. Merry Christmas," I said, which immediately felt like a really stupid thing to say to someone homeless.

"Ahh, yeh, Merry Christmas to you too, love. Have you got any change?"

"Ehh, yeh a bit," I stuttered as I fished about in my bag for my purse. "Have you been out all night?" Again, probably another silly question to ask.

"Yeh, I have." The voice belonged to a bearded face that had emerged from the rags. "It's not been too bad though, the party revellers kept me going till about 5am and one even gave me his half-drunk bottle of Whiskey so that kept me warm for a bit. It's cold now though, ehhh."

"Yes, it is," I said from the comfort of my full-length winter coat.

It was then that I noticed quite a few other people sitting in shop doorways and on the Town Centre benches, wearing the dishevelled clothes of the homeless, clutching their dirty blankets around themselves to try and keep out the cold. There were also several other people wandering aimlessly around, mainly elderly, and smartly dressed, looking lost and lonely as they peered into shop windows and gazed at the lights, passing the time of day by occasionally acknowledging one another with a sad perfunctory nod of the head. It was as if they recognised that they weren't the only ones who had nowhere to be or no one to be with on Christmas Day; and yes, they understood that was sad and depressing. No wonder the statistics say that there are more suicides this time of year than at any other. I felt crushed, like all the air had been squeezed out of my lungs and I couldn't quite catch my breath; shocked, I couldn't believe that this sadness had been under my nose for the whole year, and I was only seeing it now for the first time. Disgusted that it had taken me to be sick, miserable, and alone before I noticed it at all. I wanted to go and get a mini-bus, scoop everybody up and take them somewhere we could all have a nice big jolly-old Christmas together. Somewhere we'd be warm and toasty in front of a roaring log fire, pulling crackers, stuffing our faces, drinking to excess, laughing about nothing in particular because we felt happy, loved and alive.

But I didn't. In my defence, how could I? Where would I get the mini-bus, the money for the food or even the reservation to sit with a dozen or so other people at such late notice, it was Christmas Day, everything was booked or closed, so I didn't.

Mark picked me up at 12.30 as promised and his mum made a fuss of me as usual, even wrapping up my prawn cocktail starter in Christmas paper so at least I'd have 'something' to open. The whole family lavished me with love and warmth and laughter and told me that even though Mark and I were no longer an item, as far as they were concerned, I was still family and should never forget it.

*****

I never did, nor did I ever forget about what I had seen on that cold Christmas morning almost 20 years ago. I still feel guilty about it when I see the sad and lonely faces amongst the shambles of homeless people bundled in doorways and alleyways amidst Windsor's pomp and ceremony, challenging everything we think the town stands for in their struggle to survive. Trying to appease my guilt with a coffee here and a tenner there. Guilty enough to help out at the local homeless shelter, not just at Christmas, but on a regular basis, volunteering at another deserving charity one day a month for the last 16 years, telling myself that at least I'm doing something, as small as that may be.

What about you? Is there something you can do to make a difference this Christmas?

9
Shadows of the Past
by Robyn Kayes

It was a bright, crisp day in Windsor three days before Christmas Eve, as I strolled down Peascod Street shopping for the last few presents for my family. Somehow, I found I had walked further than intended when an unusual shop window caught my eye. It was shining with Christmas lights and a few simple decorations that were oddly old-fashioned yet managed to be more interesting than the brashness in the other shops. I stopped and stared at the window, fascinated with the items, when suddenly I spotted something that drove the breath from my heart in a shocking twist of pain.

Th … that box, I thought, … it looks like … Grandma's trinket box! Why is it here?

"Are you alright, dearie?" came the concerned voice of the shopkeeper, who had rushed to open the door, as I stood there gasping for air. "Come inside and have a seat and I'll get you a nice cup of tea." Numbly, I let myself be drawn inside. The shopkeeper led me to a stool at the back of the shop, and I sat there feeling dazed, as she bustled off to make some tea.

"I saw you stop outside and then you suddenly turned so pale, I thought that something was wrong, so I came to get you inside. My name is Annie, and I have some lovely items here which are perfect for Christmas gifts."

Her voice continued soothingly, and I had a few moments to collect my thoughts as I stared at the item that had shocked me so much.

"Thank you for your help, I'm Cassie. I'm interested in the trinket box over on the stand," I said, pointing it out to her.

"Oh!" she exclaimed, "that is an interesting piece! I picked it up at an auction, along with a few boxes of decorations. Mostly quaint items, not very modern but all in good condition, and that trinket box was amongst the decorations." She picked it up and brought it over to me. I held it up to the light and it glittered as much as it had when I last saw it in my grandparents' house that fateful Christmas thirty-three years ago, when I was eight years old.

It did not have a price label and Annie said, "It will be thirty-three pounds. It seems that you have an affinity for it; you were drawn to this shop because of the power in the box!"

What an odd comment, I thought, she's a bit witchy! This is Christmas, not Halloween!

"Did you want to look at any of the other items?" She pointed to the boxes that were standing against the wall and I walked over to have a look.

The first one had some unfamiliar decorations and ornaments; however, the second one held some remarkably familiar things. Our star decorations, I thought, and I remember that angel from the Christmas tree.

"I would like to buy these decorations as well, please," I said. I had so few reminders of my grandparents that I wanted to take the opportunity to remember them.

"Of course, dearie, that will be an extra eight pounds."

"That's fine, and I would like to ask a favour of you. Please could you possibly ask the auction house where this box came from? I am almost sure these items came from my grandparents' house, and they passed away many years ago when I was a child, so I don't know what happened to the contents of their house."

"Sure, no problem, I'll contact them tomorrow. Are you staying nearby?"

"I'm staying at the Castle Hotel on the High Street. I'll come by tomorrow afternoon, to see if you've had any success with the auction house. Thank you very much for all your help!"

I paid for the trinket box and the decorations and left the shop to go back to the hotel, stopping along the way to buy the last few gifts and have a coffee.

When I got back to the hotel, I found some messages on my phone. There was one from my sister, Stella, saying that she was delayed but would arrive tomorrow morning. Then another one from Leo, my brother, and he would arrive tomorrow in time for dinner. And one from my son, saying that he would arrive around lunchtime on Christmas Eve.

I looked through my purchases – the three familiar stars, with our star connections: the star sign Leo; Stella, which is Latin for star; and the constellation Cassiopeia for my name. Grandma loved gazing at the stars from the attic windows and had encouraged my father to study the skies as a tribute to our famous ancestor, Edmond Halley. There were a few other familiar ornaments and the Christmas angel from the top of the tree. The memories flooded in.

*****

We had last been in Windsor thirty-three years ago in 1986. Twice that year: in April to watch Halley's Comet, and then for the Christmas holidays at my grandparents' home. It had been a very cold and snowy December, as we had gathered for dinner on Christmas Eve. My grandparents, my parents, my siblings, some uncles, aunts and cousins, the usual gathering of the Halley family every year, but this one would end in tragedy. We had a beautiful dinner, and then sat around the Christmas tree, singing carols. I must have fallen asleep there, but I found myself in the bed in the room that I shared with Stella when I woke up next morning.

"Christmas morning!" Leo had shouted as he came into the room, and then we got up and thought about opening presents. We heard some noise and clattering on the stairs, and went out to find the house in turmoil, with the sound of an ambulance getting louder and louder outside. We found our distressed parents in the living room, but no sign of our grandparents. Mum told us that Grandpa had passed away during the night, and then the shock of his passing had caused Grandma to have a heart attack and she died a few hours later. We left after the combined funeral, which took place two days after Boxing Day. The large family had drifted apart after that, and from then on, we had Christmases with our parents at our home in Edinburgh.

*****

After our parents passed away a few years ago, Leo, Stella and I had decided to keep the family spirit together and we always shared Christmas at one of our homes. This year was Leo's turn, but he was in the middle of a bitter divorce, so he had suggested that maybe we could spend the Christmas holiday in Windsor and try to find our grandparents' house. We had never come back to Windsor in all this time, and I had wandered around the town since I arrived here two days ago; however, things looked so different now compared to my very young memories of that terrible time, and I couldn't find the house. I had been planning to wait for Stella and Leo to arrive to see if they remembered anything, as they are older than me, but now, with the surfacing of the items that I found in the shop, we might have a chance of finding the house again.

The next day, Stella and Charles arrived with their children. I showed Stella the trinket box and the decorations and she recognised the stars, as well as the angel, and some of the other ornaments. We all had lunch together and then Stella and I walked over to the shop, while Charles took the children for a walk by the river. Annie, the shopkeeper, told me that she had only managed to find out the street name. "It's on Clarence Crescent, but that's all I could get from the auction people."

"Thank you very much for all your help, I do appreciate it!"

We left the shop and then realised that we weren't sure which way to go. A lovely couple walked by looking at the window, and I asked them for directions, which they kindly helped us with and pointed out which way to go. We walked along and found the park on Clarence Crescent. "Look, Stella, I remember this little park, we used to play here when we were children." The gate was open, and we walked through the park, and then … "Cassie, look over there, it's the house!"

We sat down on a bench, feeling very emotional as we stared at the grand old house. Suddenly the front door opened, and out stepped … Leo! He spoke to someone behind him, and then shook hands with the man following him out. Stella jumped up and ran over to them.

"Leo! Greg!" she yelled, waving her arms at them.

Greg? I thought. Oh my God … Leo's friend from school … I had such a crush!

They turned and big grins appeared on their faces as we both caught up with them.

"Hey, girls! Remember Greg, my friend from school?" said Leo. He turned to Greg and said, "Do you remember my sisters, Stella and Cassie?"

"Oh yes, of course!" exclaimed Greg, as he hugged us. I blushed as I thought back to those days.

"Leo, what are you doing here?"

"How did you find the house?"

We all laughed at the simultaneous questions, and Leo explained, "Greg is a lawyer, he worked in his father's practice, and they bought this house a few years ago to use as offices. His father was Grandma and Grandpa' lawyer, and Greg remembered the house from the days when his father visited

Grandma and Grandpa and he used to go along. So, when I mentioned that we were visiting Windsor, he told me about the house, and I arranged to come and see him today. But how did you know where the house was?"

"I found Grandma's trinket box in a shop, as well as some Christmas decorations that were very familiar, and the shopkeeper told me that she bought it at an auction, and then she got hold of the street name where the house was," I said.

"Oh! That's strange!" said Greg. "I found that box in the attic a couple of weeks ago, and brought it downstairs to my office, because I wanted to ask you about it," he said to Leo. "Then it disappeared, and I forgot about it. Anyway, I hope you will all join me for dinner tomorrow, here at the house. We have the top two floors as our home, and the practice is on the ground floor. The office is closed from tomorrow for the holidays, and I would love to catch up with all of you." He looked at me as he said that, and it seemed as though he put a special emphasis on these last words.

Leo drove us back to the hotel where we met up with Charles and the children. Then he told us that Greg had invited us all to share Christmas Eve dinner and Christmas Day lunch with him and his family, which we were surprised about, as we thought that Leo had booked dinner and lunch at the hotel. As we were chatting, my phone buzzed with a text.

"Hi, this is Greg. I got your number from Leo, and I would really like to talk to you tomorrow. Please could you come over to the house around 11 a.m."

I saved the number and replied, "Hi, yes of course, I'll see you tomorrow!"

I told Leo and Stella about the text, "What do you think he wants to talk about?"

Leo replied, "When we were talking earlier, he mentioned that he wanted to redecorate the offices, and I said that you were an interior decorator, so I think he wants to offer you a job, decorating the offices for him."

"That sounds interesting! What has Greg been up to? I thought he got married soon after leaving university."

"He did, and they had two children, one is still at school and the other is at university. His wife had cancer a few years back and she had chemotherapy. But it returned, and she died last year."

"Oh no! That's terrible!" I said, shocked. "Why didn't you tell me when it happened? I could have contacted him and wished him condolences."

"I'm sorry, Cass, it was such a shock at the time. Also, I think you were working on that job in America, and I didn't really want to bother you."

"Okay, forgiven! I'll offer my sympathies tomorrow. So, anyway, come and have a look at this stuff that I found."

I showed the trinket box and the ornaments to Leo, and he recognised the stars and some of the animal ornaments. As he was looking at the trinket box, holding it up to the light, I was reminded of a time when I saw Grandma hold it up the same way and then, when she opened the lid, it must have had a secret compartment, because I seem to remember seeing some paper folded up in the hidden space. I took the box and held it up the same way that I remembered Grandma holding it, whilst gently feeling around for some sort of switch.

"Got it!" I exclaimed as the little door was released, and there was the paper folded up inside. I tugged it out and opened it. "It's a letter from Grandma!" I said, showing it to them. We all gathered around to read it.

To my Darling Stars Leo, Stella, and Cassiopeia. I hope that you are having a lovely Christmas holiday. I have hidden some presents for you in a special hiding place. Follow the Stars which lead the way. Enjoy! Lots of Love, Grandma.

We were all stunned, and then we wondered why she had done this and where they could be. "We can ask Greg tomorrow whether we could have a look around and see if we can find anything," said Leo.

After this excitement, we went out for dinner and tried to talk about other things.

*****

The next morning, I walked over to the house. I was feeling very apprehensive about going in, because of the bad memories, but as Greg opened the front door and I walked in, I could see that it looked very different from how I remembered it. There was a tall lady standing in the front room who looked vaguely familiar, and Greg introduced me to his aunt, Tabitha.

"Hello, my dear," she said. "How lovely to see you again; I remember you when you were a child. And I met your brother Leo yesterday when he visited Greg. I worked as the housekeeper here for your grandparents, and now I am the office manager for Greg's practice, as well as looking after the house for him. And I have a confession to make to both of you. I gave that box of decorations to Annie, my sister who owns the gift shop," she said to me. "We knew that you would be drawn to it, because of the power of the trinket box."

Another 'power' comment, I thought, she's also witchy!

"Your grandmother wanted you to have it, but somehow, it must have fallen into the box of decorations when we took down the tree all those years ago. It all landed up in the attic, and we forgot about it till now."

"Oh! How strange!" I said.

"Aunt Tabitha, will you please bring some tea to the office, I want to talk to Cassie," said Greg, as he showed me into his office. "Please have a seat," he said, and I sat down near the window, my mind in a whirl of memories as I looked around the room, while Greg sat down near me and continued, "I did wonder how the shopkeeper knew where the house was, but as it was Annie, she got the box from here and not from the auctioneers. So, what do you think about the house?"

"This room looks quite different from what I remember; it's all painted white. I suppose that was done for the offices," I said.

"Yes, that's something I wanted to talk to you about. I mentioned to Leo that the offices needed some sprucing up, and I want it to look more like it did before. Also, I wanted to update the top floors where I live with my family. Leo told me that you are an interior decorator, so I would like you to consider taking on the redecorating job."

"Oh, that sounds interesting! I would love to take it on and spend some time in the house. I've just finished decorating an office building in London, and I decided to take some time off, to have a break before my next assignment. I could get started in January."

"I'm using the ground floor as offices, and then the first floor is where I live, with my two children, and Aunt Tabitha has the second floor, with Aunt Annie and her husband, Uncle Harold, and then there are the attics above them. Leo might have told you that my wife passed away last year from cancer, and then the Aunts and Uncle Harold moved in to help us." His eyes shone with tears, and I touched his arm to comfort him. He gulped and then cleared the emotion with a cough.

"I'm so sorry, Greg! I didn't know any of that, I was working on an assignment in America last year, and Leo only told me what had happened last night."

"Tea, anyone!" came the welcome sound of Tabitha, rattling the tea trolley.

"Thanks, I'll have it black, with lemon," said Greg, "How about you, Cassie?"

"I'll have mine with milk and one sugar, thanks," I said. "And these biscuits look delicious, did you make them, Tabitha?"

"Oh, Annie does the cooking and baking, and I look after the practice for Greg, and the rest of the house and the kids," she said. "It all keeps me busy! Now, Greg, have you told Cassie about Christmas?"

"Ah, yes, I was coming to that," he said. "I spoke to Leo, and he was going to speak to all of you. I would like you all to come here for Christmas Eve dinner, as well as Christmas Day lunch. I know you have bad memories of that time when your grandparents passed away, and I hope that you will be able to make some new, good memories with us. We are also trying hard to come to terms with things, and we would really enjoy having all of you over to distract us from our thoughts and fill the house with some joy and Christmas spirit."

"Thank you, Greg, and Tabitha, it sounds like a lovely idea! And we'll all help with the cooking."

"Here's Annie," said Tabitha, as Annie came into the room.

"Hi Cassie," said Annie, "sorry about the deception, we knew you were in Windsor, as we had seen it in the cards, and I knew you would be drawn to my shop by the power in the box."

"That's okay, Aunts," said Greg. "Aunt Annie, we would like a light lunch at one o'clock, maybe some sandwiches," as he ushered them out of the office, "and now we can continue our discussion."

"Are those two witches? They sound like it with 'seeing it in the cards' and the 'power of the box'," I smiled.

"They love pretending, I try hard to ignore all that nonsense," he said.

"How does Annie manage to do the cooking as well as run the gift shop?"

"She is only there part-time, as Uncle Harold mostly runs it. We can look around the offices first, and then I'll show you upstairs. The house is very solid, so it wouldn't need any alteration to the structure, it's only the rooms that need some work. I was thinking of some wood panelling, and new carpets and curtains. And maybe some more on the upper floors."

"I'll make some notes about the rooms and what you think should be done, and I can then work on it and come up with some suggestions. There was something else that I wanted to ask you about … in that trinket box, we found a letter from Grandma, which said that she had hidden some presents for us in a secret hiding place. Do you think maybe we could have a look around this evening?"

"Of course, we can all join in and make it a treasure hunt, the kids will love it! I've got the original plans of the house in my office, we can have a look at those first, and see if it shows any secret rooms or passageways."

"That's fantastic! I would need to see the plans anyway for the redecorating."

I had extensive notes about the rooms by lunchtime, when we sat down to a delicious meal of soup and sandwiches made with home-baked bread. We stayed there for a while, chatting, and catching up over coffee. Greg walked back to the hotel with me, and we met up with Leo and Stella.

"I'll see you all later around six o'clock," said Greg, as he left us.

"I told Greg about the letter, and he said we could have a treasure hunt this evening. I had a look at the plans of the house, but I couldn't see anywhere that it could be."

"Don't worry, Cass, I'm sure we'll find them. What about the decorating, did he ask you?"

"Yes, and I said I would take it on. I can start in January, when Collin goes back to school."

"Sounds great," said Leo.

"I had a thought about the letter," I said, taking it out of my handbag. "It says 'Follow the Stars which lead the way.' That

must be a reference to how to get to the hiding place. The three stars that were part of the decorations … they had our names with diagrams of the constellations, that could be the pathway. And look at how the 's' of 'Stella' is written, it's got four little circles on it. That must be part of the pathway. Your star has your name
written with the circles, like in the letter."

"Yes," said Stella. "Maybe we should start in the attics, I remember that there were a lot of nooks and crannies up there."

"Yes, that's possible," I said. "The box of decorations was up there. We can have a look around tonight."

*****

"Let's just check that everything is in place in the attic, Annie," said Tabitha. "We must make sure that the instructions are followed exactly as our letter from Mrs Halley said. It's time they received the gifts their Grandma wanted them to have - they were her favourite grandchildren. Their uncle did his best to block the family from getting their rightful inheritance, he was always very jealous. He got the family business and the house, and the contents should have gone to his brother Edward, and his children, but he sold everything, except for the things that were hidden away."

Christmas is Coming
By June Kerr

Christmas is coming
And I'm certainly getting fat
Sitting on the sofa
In my poky little flat

Stuffing in the Quality Street
From a tub the size of Mars
Eating dates and walnuts
In between the chocolate bars

Drinking little sherries
From a glass my grandma left
In between the lagers
And the wine and all the rest

Pondering when 12th night is
And when the Sales will all begin
Ordering a curry
As I finish off the gin

Wondering where my neighbours are
My family and my friends
Feeling lost and lonely
And wishing it would end

Loneliness seems so much worse
As Christmas comes around
Questioning what the point is
As I sit piling on the pounds

Contemplating suicide
The where's, the how's, the why's
Something not too gory
As I wipe tears from my eyes

Wish I had the strength
To end the misery and the pain
Cause if I don't I'll feel the same
When Christmas comes again

Bear a thought for those of us
For whom Christmas is so sad
Perhaps a call or friendly word
Could turn it good from bad

Suicides at Christmas
Are the highest of the year
Is there someone you could help
With a dose of Christmas cheer?

10
To Bite the Hand That Feeds
By Kanthè

The Kingdom

Once upon a time, in a kingdom not too far removed from this one, there stood a great tall castle on a hill. It overlooked a flat plain of land through which a lazy river of greens and blues and naked hues flowed. This snaked around the base of the hillock upon which the castle is still perched. Like the river, the stone edifice of this citadel changes colour with the mood of the day.

Alongside the river, down one side, is nestled the town known as *Windles-Ore*. It has a history running back to the Dark Ages. The town rises up from the river, to the ramparts of the castle like reaching hands. The very model of deference and respectability.

At the same time, however, scandal sheets are read throughout this town. There is a selection that you can choose from any newsagent - from the national gutter rags to the upmarket broadsheets that appear almost respectable.

The biggest scandal sheet in the land is *The Daily Chainmail*. An odd name, for sure. Of course, no one wears chainmail anymore. So, it is a paper for another time and another place (a place long gone). A paper concerned with the price of property (and the size of one's portfolio) but the value of precisely ... nothing. It's always talking about England's Dreaming – a yearning for a time long gone.

But nonetheless, it puts on its chainmail armour – ready to go into battle, like a dutiful general. It's always going to fight the good fight. To bat for the status quo.

It is a paper that tries to create its own reality. A fairytale of its own, if you will – as perfectly illustrated as a Ladybird book. With its own cod-morality, its own hierarchy, its own system of beliefs. At the top of that belief system is not The Church – it is The Castle and The Crown.

The castle stands tall and resolute. Dark and sombre against a moody sky – the slate-coloured stones the same; like the traditional house haunted upon the hill, but just bigger and bolder. Full of the past – absolutely reeking of it. Heritage and tradition - the rock it is perched upon. It all screams conformity, conformity … and the punishment of non-conformity.

But the castle is haunted by the ghosts of mad Kings, disreputable Princes, and drunken Princesses. All echoing within the long, lonely passages inside. It is sumptuous but cold inside. A murder to heat in winter – I've been told.

A cool, detached atmosphere pervades the place all year round. Settling around its structure like a shroud of respectability.

Far below the base of the castle, on the side of the hillock away from the town, lies The Enchanted Forest. This is a dark, magical place that wraps itself around the rising earth in various shades of verdant green, but it is plagued by packs of wolves. They are always hungry – ravenous, in fact. They are always circling the castle – looking for scraps – any mishaps, so they can pounce, devour, and kill. Then maybe even resurrect your mistakes and pounce and devour and kill them all over again.

There is a legend that these hungered creatures were human once – in the dim and distant past. Now you cannot tell them from the other beasts that prowl by night. The bears and foxes that wander into town.

Times have changed in this land. The quiet plague of a silent enemy enshrouds everyone. We are now living in a world much more risk-averse – scared of itself and its consequences. The people are cowered behind masks.

There was a time when a king would lead his army into battle;
be willing to die for his country – but those days are long gone. In today's world, royalty is not even allowed to stub their toe in the field of battle. Leave that to the plebeian classes – that's what they're there for.

Today the battles are fought and won in the press – in the court of public opinion. Again, the royals don't take part, officially; but again, it is done in their name. It's always the *friends of friends*; *hidden sources* to sling the barbs. They can't be seen to get involved – not in the blood-shed, not in the shit-flinging.

They have to save face. Perhaps things have not changed that much after all.

The Two Princesses in the Tower

Inside the castle are sat two princesses – up in the tower. They stare out of different windows in different directions. The windows are both gilded but locked. One of the princesses is known as White Rose, the other is Black Thorn.

They have a few things in common. Both are roughly the same age. Both are Outsiders – both are known as commoners by the courtiers and associated hangers-on that litter the place. The people that think they are In *The Know* – the so-called 'anonymous sources' for the stories that burn through this place and end up in the scandal rags.

The vipers in this collective bosom.

The stories that are published about these two have to be seen to be unbelieved. Great reams of useless drivel that is written about them. Enough to keep a whole industry of feckless people afloat. You wonder how this industry survived before these two women came into the royal circle.

They are the newest members to join The Family. Join – rather than be born into it. They should be like sisters; two sisters from another mother – but they are not. Neither had a life prior to becoming princess, not really; or if they had, it has been sanitised. Homogenised. Packaged and repackaged. It is there, but never really referred to.

Well, that is the idea – and White Rose has a life that follows this narrow trajectory. The route to being the fairy atop this Christmas tree. Her future is decided ... clear-cut. She is not one to rock the boat – to wander off the path. There is no real delving into her past. Or if there is – it's an overwhelmingly positive coverage.

The same is not true for Black Thorn – her past is brought up all the time. Her position, her future, is still an unknown. And maybe because of that, they tear into her past. Maybe the wolves just don't like her – they want to tear into her history: where she was born, where she was raised. The people she grew up with – the people she hangs with.

*****

White Rose likes looking at the river flowing from the West. From the direction of her home. The river changes colour in the failing light like the mood of her eyes.

No hint of a sexual past for her, of course. It has all been air-brushed out. Her role has been secured. She is the official 'baby-making machine'. To secure *an heir ... and a spare* is the inane phrase that is used. No hint of individuality, a personality, an outburst – no kind of passion is allowed to remain. All the

117

creases and wrinkles ironed out. It is all about duty … duty … and even more duty. It is a shroud that enfolds her all - every day of every week.

A good princess is a mute princess. That was advice that came right from the very top.

White Rose looks at herself in the gilded mirror. It is amazing how her skin looks smoother than a year before. Less of the lines and imperfections … more of the plastic inevitable. She practises her sincere smile in the mirror. It is her most valuable asset.

*****

Black Thorn looks sharply to the East. She thinks that calm and meditative philosophies will help her. Bring about a *New Her*. Maybe it can be something that she can sell – but it won't. It won't give her respite. It won't save her ... from the fall – when it will inevitably come … in the Fall.

They call her Black Thorn because she is sharp, pushy … and prickly, of course. Sharp and pushy because of the country she was born into - and her previous job; a job of mild glamour. It gave her various roles to play, various roles with various names. Such names, of course, are mild compared to what she is called in the scandal rags today. Everything from *Witch* to *Bitch* it seems - stains the pages.

Now *she* is one to wander off the winding path. To take a walk in The Enchanted Forest - on her own; to bring something back. To take further steps into the unknown - which makes her an *Unknown*. An unknown quantity is a dangerous thing.

Especially in this land - in this family.

Previous unknown quantities have caused consternation and embarrassment. They have had to be …discreetly removed.

*****

From somewhere down below in The Enchanted Forest - there is the howl of a lone wolf. Then another ... and another - on a cold, still night it travels. Soon it is the howl of the wolf-pack. The last one sounds so close - almost as if it were coming from inside the castle.

Imagine that - *a Wolf inside the castle*?

It causes Black Thorn to shiver and pull her bed-clothes tighter around her. Sometimes she likes to lie in bed at night staring at the white ceiling. Looking at the patterns forming and unforming around her like a play.

The legend of Little Red Riding Hood has always scared her. The idea of a young girl lost in a forest; the idea of a big shaggy man-wolf with a lupine grin. Saliva - thick and non-oily dripping between savage canines. She can't help thinking:

Would she be attacked? ... would she be eaten? Consumed. Destroyed.

She falls into an uneasy sleep...

Black Thorn's Dream

...And falls into a well of wild dreams. Of running in a moonlit forest - The Enchanted Forest painted blue-silver. The trees like angry black shadows rushing towards her - catching and ripping at her clothes. Whispering fervid questions at her. Lights popping. There is another howl somewhere behind her - it is close, very close; too close.

Now there is a growl - and a cough, and an almost childish splutter. It sounds almost human. An animalistic man ...*a werewolf?*

The next morning, she wakes in a cold stupor. A dread pervades the place as she greets her in-laws. They are all there: her father-in-law ...tall and angular; his sister the same but doughty. His brother - more rotund and jovial - lumbering and awkward in his own skin. He has the wolf's grin; wolfish, of course...but sheepish too - to comfort the sheep, the little lambs … before he leaps on them. Devours them.

The shock - shocks Black Thorn out of her dream. She is back in the bloodied tower.

To Bite the Hand That Feeds

The next day looks like any other day - like today. Both of them look like White Rose and Black Thorn - looking like two virginal babes up in the tower. Fully made up and dressed to the nines with fake smiles for the people outside. Like showroom dummies on display. The castle is barbed and guarded by many men with automatic weapons. Very nervous men.

In the past it would have been with swords and spears and whatnots. But these days it is semi-automatic weaponry that keeps everybody secure ... but not necessarily safe.

Sometimes, the two princesses feel like rare birds - both with a fine crystal plumage - but a different coloured plumage. It's something that a lot of people admire and want to see and copy. However, beautiful things should not be kept in a cage (even a gilded one) - to be gawked at by the public. Prodded and poked for a reaction.

No creature would like to be displayed like that. Not even a normally passive, easy- going one. It might well ... *bite the hand that feeds.*

*****

White Rose is still looking at herself in the mirror.

She is looking more and more like her favourite character from a fairytale. Her hair is as black as ebony, skin as soft and white as the purest snow. She even has the blood- red lipstick that she uses sparingly - so as not to wear out that image.

Everything has to be relaxed, effortless. She has to be calm personified - the perfect English Rose. That nothing can be allowed to disturb. Like white, virginal snow ... undisturbed.

Every girl wants to be Snow White.

But care should be taken when taking on this role. A girl can only play Snow White for a very short period of her life.

121

You can't hold onto that innocence for any length of time. You stay in the role too long and you end up playing the Snow Queen.

Despite all the efforts to the contrary, she can see the lines that weren't there before. Minute lines around the eyes and the corner of the mouth like crow's feet. She frowns - one single white hair (slightly kinked) off her centre-parting catches the fading light. She plucks it out.

The thought that enters her mind is this: *What happens when you're too old to be a Princess?* Are you allowed to grow out of it - the public perception?

The worry she does not articulate is repeated: If you spend time, too long as a Princess, there is a danger that you go from White Rose ...to Snow Queen...to Ice Queen...to Ice Maiden. Her soft green eyes harden at the thought.

She wonders how people see her. Could she be the new Queen of Hearts ...one day?

Would *They* let her?

When White Rose falls asleep, she dreams about the things she can't really talk about.

White Rose's Dream

In her dream, she is always approaching a big imposing house - dark and forbidding on the hill as evening approaches. The last house on her list. There is a big dark mahogany door; almost blood-red in colour - studded by thick dusty metal nails and a big lion's head knocker. She initially thinks it's brass like the small knocker on her parent's house - like the one on her student flat door at university; but on closer examination she is surprised to find out that this one is actually made of solid gold. A gold lion with a ring through its nose. She caresses the ring as if in love.

She's about to knock using the heavy gold knocker - almost as a last resort; when the door swings open in total silence - like the sound has suddenly been cut from the world. She doesn't want to go in, not really - but her parents and sister are standing behind her on the lush midnight lawn in their Sunday best. A summer sun on their midnight faces. Encouraging smiles on their faces - eager and bright. An encouragement to go on...*go on ...go on.*

She finally does ... walking a long, narrow, dark passageway that opens into a great hall with a high ceiling and chandeliers and red plush furniture. Rather grand - like that massive dining hall in those Harry Potter films.

There is a pure white unicorn that is being led around the room by a blonde-haired woman in a red evening gown and a red blindfold. This woman is holding a white dove in one hand and the unicorn via a gold coloured, silk knotted rope in the other. There is a man wearing a purple hood and carrying a massive fire axe. The unicorn kneels down before the man in the hood as he raises the axe. The dove disappears.

Rather disconcerted, White Rose backs out of the hall but now she's at the back of the building and there is a car parked outside under a circle of blazing security lights. It is fully night now.

The car is a jet-black limousine, which reflects back the haloes of the lights - a Mercedes Benz S20 the driver tells her in a reassuring voice. He's a bespectacled, stocky French man and he mutters *in vino veritas* as he ushers her into the back. There are two mannequins on the back seat and one in the front passenger seat. Three solid plastic bodies with hazard strips on the impassive faces.

She looks out into the night and there is the wolf pack on the very edge of the forest that borders this building. Their shadowy figures bleeding out of the night flora and fauna. Silhouetted against the navy of the night sky. The only natural light burns like flames where their eyes should be.

The guy in the glasses is now in the driver's seat and floors the Mercedes into the night. Of course, the wolf pack gives chase - running behind and alongside the vehicle. Yapping and showing their teeth. Their eyes now white - pure white and snapping and flashing at her as she clings to the inside door handle. The lights - bouncing off the car. The night rushes out at her, through the twisty streets of Windles-Ore they go - getting faster and faster.

Down past the river - lit up, even at this time of night. Snow flurries funnel in the air. Then they bank left under the looming railway viaduct that looks like a tunnel and then a tight turn on the roundabout onto the road out of town.

Now they are on the dual carriageway heading towards the motorway. The wolves still there behind them in dogged pursuit - they know all the short-cuts. Unable to shake them off, the car goes even faster - lurching forward towards a small black hole that gets bigger and bigger - the faster they approach it. Soon it is all White Rose can see - a cartoon-like thick yawning black hole on a solid structure towards which the limousine is hurtling.

She wakes just before the car slams into the solid black hole.

History Repeating

White Rose meets Black Thorn at the base of the Round Tower. A tower that is not quite round. - like most things to do with royalty - nothing is really as it seems. They stare at each other for a long time. Soft green eyes meet chocolate brown.

They look warily at each other ...circling around. Like two similar creatures that can't see the similarities between themselves. The stiffness of the body language says it all. As if one was spots and the other was stripes and that's all there was to it. Who was a threat to whom? Who could say?

At times - both wondered: *…who was the better actress?*

White Rose wears a long red coat - quite long and classy and well cut with big brass soldier buttons on it. It has a wide, deep hood which she hardly ever wears up. Black Thorn doesn't like it - it irks her. The question on her mind is: *Who does she think she is ... Little Red Riding Hood?*

Black Thorn of course wears black - an equally long black coat and maybe a pair of scarlet gloves. White Rose doesn't like this. She glowers behind her winsome smile.

Was this Interloper having a dig? Was there blood on her hands? … blood on her tracks?

There are a few snow flurries in the air. The air has turned cold between them.

They are heading inexorably towards the end of the year.

*****

You would think that at Christmas - a season of goodwill and cheer things would change. But they do not.

Black Thorn looks out of the window of the Round Tower. It is another day full of snow. It smothers everything - the shops on the High Street ...making it look like a proper Christmas scene.

She looks down to see White Rose far below in her long red coat and hood - spread like a growing bloodstain on the virgin snow, like a poppy flowering in a dream of white. Again, the thought: *Who does she think she is...?*

They both think about their parents:

The mothers of both are to be admired - but criticised too: i.e., be kept in their place. The fathers are invisible or widely considered as a joke or to be used, if anything, as a weapon.

In fairy tales, fathers are usually noblemen – but fathers are not important in fairy tales. The fathers of these two women have been separated, marginalized, kept in the shadows, not treated like noble men. It is as if they have done their job and are not wanted or needed anymore.

*****

These princesses should both beware of the past. Contrary to popular opinion, their future is not secure. Princesses have disappeared in the past. Both physically disappeared and metaphorically – been sidelined into the shadows. Persona non-grata, an embarrassment, not to be mentioned in polite company.

Christmas

Black Thorn looks at the picture of a pale man on a cross. He has such white skin, blue eyes, and long blond hair. That is how he is portrayed in films and paintings. A European face in a Middle Eastern setting. The same with the sculpted figure on the large cross in the castle's chapel.

She can see how people like to reinvent people. Reinvent themselves. This was a staple thing where she was from. The Land of her Fathers, that massive land beyond the unfathomable sea. An ocean of turmoil existed between the two worlds.

It disturbs her with a vision:

She is inside a very small room with a narrow sloping ceiling that is more cupboard than room. She is looking at the man on the cross again, but he is old and wizened now, his body almost reddish-brown. Almost native American. The face is the same colour – it looks drawn and haggard and horribly aged. The glorious blonde locks are now a frizzy dried-out auburn thatch on his head. The eyes that were supplicant but open to God are now wide and staring and lit with a corrupted zeal. The light of this corruption shines out like an energy-saving bulb inside the head. Inside with one good idea. The head turns and looks at Black Thorn with eyes ablaze.

Black Thorn is there inside this cupboard room and the door to her left (the only way out) has a nasty big split running from top to bottom. As if someone has taken a bloody big axe to it. As if it was the symbol, the very essence of impotent rage and fury.

How she wished there was another door at the back of this cupboard/wardrobe room, a means to escape through. Or maybe if she kept walking back and back and back ... she would pass by rows of wintery coats hung up – some even with dandruff like snowflakes that are cold to the touch. Walking back and back until she ends up ankle--deep in fresh snow – in some wintery woods ... away into another world. Maybe one more benign than the one she left.

The vision, like the snow, dissolves.

Black Thorn secretly enjoyed reading the Daily Chainmail. She never would if anyone else were around – but on her own, she could indulge herself. Her motto growing up was 'Know Thy Enemy!' and she knew this enemy very well.

The coverage of royalty in the Chainmail is unbelievable: What they are doing. What they are wearing (where you could order it for yourself). What the grandchildren are wearing. Like the creepy uninvited guest at a birthday party.

The question she wanted to ask was *Why*? Why do you care? You're never going to be invited around. Never going to be part of that Inner Circle. The answer, of course, was ownership. The Chainmail wanted people to know that *they* owned royalty; could do with it what they wanted.

And the Daily Chainmail was the Will of the People, its own people.

One winter-sun day, in the run up to Christmas, Black Thorn ventures out of the castle into town. Onto Peascod Street. They call it a walkabout – out amongst the people, a Meet and Greet, if you will.

She is disturbed to see the shops that normally sell royal trinkets and tacky souvenirs are now selling masks with her face on it. Empty eye-sockets and a frozen smile hanging up in bunches. These are then taken up by the blank, smiling masses, now wearing her smiling face ... with blue/green eyes where her brown eyes should have been. They approach around her. She backs slowly away.

Transformation

Transformation is key to all fairy tales. It's about growing up, changing. In fairy tales transformation is just a matter of Will. You think it, you are it. You are whatever you identify as being.

In the real world of the here and now, it takes more blood, sweat and tears to get what you want – to get the change you want. Change comes at a price – sometimes the price is too high.

Princesses, of course, are ripe for transformation. They are growing up - growing into a new role, with a growing responsibility. They can somehow see the future ahead.

Do they want it? … Or do they want to change?

Black Thorn's Transformation

On the morning of Christmas Eve, Black Thorn's boot-prints are found in the crisp virgin snow which lies thick at the inclining base of the West Tower. They are heading out towards the Albert Memorial Chapel. They stop at a small hole in the snow which is filled with blood and one of her red gloves lies nearby.

The people that find it are suitably aghast. Dainty female footprints run on the other side of the hole and then … just stop. There is nothing else there but the jet-black tail feather of a raven.

Black Thorn is never seen again.

White Rose's Transformation

White Rose keeps her doubts and insecurities better hidden. But they are there nonetheless, still a princess in name only. Despite the baubles, still an outsider only.

White Rose's transformation takes longer because it requires a degree of new learning.

But she is no dummy … No Waity-Katie like one of her friends. She looks and observes. She has heard Black Thorn's pacings, her whispered incantations at night through the tower walls. She has access to the same books, the Internet – the same grit more deeply hidden. The same commitment, less resolved.

So, she says the words. Draws the lines and diagrams on her bedroom wall in red chalk. She cries; she paces. The same puddle of blood on the floor.

Nothing happens.

Then one day she looks in the mirror and sees her skin has started to mottle. And goose bumps start to rise up on the surface of her legs like goose flesh. Like she is suddenly cold; unwanted, rejected. Like somebody has walked over her grave.

Her interest in fashion changes from the entirely functional and clean and Home Counties appeal to something more esoteric. She develops an interest in feathers – of all things; white, of course. She presses them against herself as she arches her neck rather like an inquisitive turtledove, in her gilded mirror. There is an orange stain around her mouth. She screams and runs out of the tower, as if on fire.

White Rose just makes it to the river. She wanders in the cold, silvery waters that run past the castle. She no longer feels the cold; she is her usual serene self as she moves through the dark waters, upstream, heading for home. The feet moving frantically below the waterline; while her body glides along above the surface, undisturbed.

Can this be true?

On the edge of the town, she looks back, she thinks she has made it; there is no one behind her. She looks at herself in the still grey waters of winter. A mute swan with an orange bill stares back at her. She stares at herself in fear and admiration ... and terror.

The joy that there is magic in the world is good. But the horror of realising that this is NOT what she wanted. All magic is a negotiation with outside forces, and she has just lost it, Big Time.

For all mute swans are owned by The Crown.

The Queen looks out across the icy river with her binoculars but quite rightly says not a word.

11
Miss Bunne Takes a Trip
By Helena Marie

Of all things, at this time what Miss Bunne really wants is a hand to hold, for somebody to be there. She sits straight backed, ankles neatly crossed, handbag on her lap. The door opens,
an usher runs his finger down a clipboard, and she readies to stand, but he doesn't call her name. The only woman here; she observes the walls giving backbone to the young men slouching against them. Of all things, all she wants is a hand to hold, for somebody – no, not just somebody – for Jim, to be there, to understand. Exhaling, she considers how a moment's decision has brought her here.

*****

For 54 years, Miss Bunne had, in most regards, remained unblemished. In her long career, she had been an example to others; her exemplary students and irregular methods inspired those eager to emulate her success. So revered was she that many of those young students forgot that she was more than just Miss Bunne, assuming that she began and ended at the school gates, and in some ways they were right. But not in all. Eileen (as she was known to her peers) led a solitary life, but not one without amusement. The bridge and tennis clubs, the walking group: all had the benefit of her company, and a fine companion she was. An occupied mind, she believed, was a healthy mind and   she was nothing if not diligent in her efforts, but this hadn't always been her life.

Many years before, Miss Bunne had married Jim, her best friend and soulmate. This little-known fact was not so much a secret to be hidden, as a constant wound to soothe with movement, activity, distraction. They lived a happy life of safety and comfort, talking and loving, road trips and favourite places. And it was this that she missed the most: the days spent driving in the cab of an old Morris Minor, a special place they'd made their own. She had sold the car eventually, when the shock of his death had become manageable and the estate settled, and she had understood that to go on living was the only way to honour him. She packed up their house, gave the clothes he'd worn to charity, moved to Windsor and found a job in a different school. Miss Bunne refused the title her marriage could have claimed, not to obliterate Jim's memory, but to guard it from questions; instead holding it in the sanctity of secrecy, away from the pain caused by others' curiosity. And so, life began again, but deep down she knew that a piece of her heart was forever lost between the seats of that musty old green car.

Feet were Miss Bunne's mode of choice in those new days; her house a brisk walk from school, she combined walking with work and found both pleasant enough. Modern cars were boxes that she passed as she crossed the car park to her class. Routine soothed her; she felt comfort in schedules and the expected.

"Stop running, Diggins."

"Sorry, Miss."

She opened her classroom door, crossed to the window, lifted the sash, and breathed in.

Turning away, she felt a sudden compulsion to go back and take in the view. The familiar snub nose and bonnet hadn't registered at first but there it was: a car just like she and Jim had owned, its window half open as if extending an invitation.

She checked herself. Vehicles like that were oddities these days, but even so, it sat in its bay, as real as all the others. Miss Bunne remembered their car: the cracked leather of the seats, the wooden wheel under her gloved hand, the smell of the hot engine. Not normally given to reminiscing, she was undefended against its pull, but still, just once she stood and let herself recall.

"Miss? There's a man here to see you."

She hadn't heard the door, or the prefect with a guest, and with the smallest shake of her head, she turned back to the room.

"Thank you, Stephen."

She greeted the man, "Good morning. Can I help you?"

"Hello. I'm here to fix the projector."

"Oh, at last, that is good news. Let me show you where it is."

*****

The day was long as midweek always was; English Language, then Literature, and when she could, marking and feedback and setting assignments, yet Miss Bunne was unsettled, as though a part of her had unmoored. The structure that soothed her had tilted and she couldn't seem to right it. Probably best to call it a day, so she began to tidy her desk. Dusk was overtaking the afternoon as she strode across the car park, but enough was left to show the classic car, chrome work shining under the security light. Miss Bunne could see boxes on the rear seat, a reminder of picnics and rugs, their just-in-case umbrella. At least it's a well-used car, she thought, and carried on her way.

*****

Winter nights lengthened as the end of term approached. Miss Bunne had hoped to see the car again, but she was disappointed: instead, headlights were halogen-bright, engines ran quietly, batteries held charge. Once, walking home, she thought she recognised the rounded stack of rear lights as a car drove past, but it was swallowed up in winter gloom, and she told herself it was just coincidence.

*****

January arrived. First day back was always busy, bittersweet with other people's Christmas memories, and students struggling to reconcile themselves to timetables. By the second lesson it was becoming obvious that not everything had appreciated the break: water was dripping in the women's toilet, and the projector seemed intent on taking extended leave. Miss Bunne put in a request for repairs and worked around the inconvenience. Soon enough the rhythm of routine asserted itself as the school slipped into its well-honed ways, and Stephen once again brought a guest to class. This time Miss Bunne was sitting, considering grades, when the door opened. She greeted them both, thanked the boy and showed the man the erratic projector, asking, "Was that your Morris Minor I saw in the car park before?"

He looked caught off guard; perhaps more used to this from a man.

"Yes, it is. Do you know them?"

"Yes. Well, I used to. I had one but it was a long time ago. I haven't seen one in many years, that's all."

She left the words hanging, aware that an innocent comment could stir up thoughts she didn't want to own, and turned back to her desk.

The man worked quietly, and Miss Bunne kept a keen eye on the clock. It was almost time to pack up and go home to warmth and food and reading by sidelight, but still the man was hunched over the projector.

"I'm so sorry to interrupt but school finishes shortly and I'll need to close the classroom. Do you think you'll be much longer?"

"Another half an hour should do it. I just need to replace some wires and test it; I don't want it to break again."

"No, of course. Will you be alright if I leave you here? I'm so sorry, but I do need to get away."

He didn't look up.

"Yes, that's fine. I'll let the headmaster know when I'm done."

That was all Miss Bunne needed. Tidying her papers, she set the desk to rights and said a polite goodbye. Walking down the dim corridor, she wondered what sort of person would drive a car so old these days.

Most of the teachers had already left and the car park was almost empty, apart from the Morris. Miss Bunne walked closer than needed to the car, telling herself she could look, just for nostalgia, for Jim. It was dark inside and there wasn't much to see, but her eye was caught by a glint in the grey – a key, still in the ignition.

"How very careless," she thought, "I suppose I should go back and tell him. Better still, I'll take him the keys."

Putting her hand on the pitted handle, she gave a gentle pull and smelled the scent of years gone by.

For all her good intentions, Miss Bunne glanced quickly around the car park, saw that nobody was there and with the familiarity of countless journeys, took her place behind the wheel. How odd to feel so at home, as though no time had passed at all. The solidity of the steering wheel, the gear stick under her palm; she remembered Jim and the thrill of setting off, their destination to be found as the mood took them. Surely one small turn around the car park couldn't do any harm.

The Morris was clearly well loved; its engine fired first time and with practise and precision, she slipped into reverse, straightened up, found first gear, and pulled out of the bay. The classroom window remained empty, the engineer no doubt still bent over his work. A nice man, he wouldn't mind, she thought. Changing smoothly to second gear, Miss Bunne found a joy she thought would never be hers again. The car was keen, ready to go; it just needed space and a good trip to do it justice. Approaching the school gates, she turned to go back to the bay, and in a moment's compulsion, pulled instead onto the road. Breath shortened and heart pumping, she reached forward, muscle memory taking over as she put the headlights on. The school shrank in the rear-view mirror, as Miss Bunne headed north, to the M4 and the past.

As the car worked its magic, Miss Bunne remembered all the things she had stowed away: Jim's profile, the way he would tell her "Watch that car, Eileen," the crack of cold air and the window winder, the tick of the indicator and the glow of the lights, the bounce of suspension on the tarmac. She drove with purpose, and as the miles erased the years, she had no concern for what she'd done.

Navigating the roads as though she'd never been off them, Eileen Bunne needed nothing more than memory to guide her from the suburbs of Windsor, through the green of Berkshire, the industry of Swindon, the signs counting down to Bristol. But there was no call for her there; instead, she left the motorway and took the A46 to Bath, that place of mellow stone and Georgian elegance, vivid with memories of Jim.

On the outskirts of the city, finding a space, she reversed in, aligned the car with the kerb, and turned off the engine. There was no urgency to leave, it was enough to sit for now in the warm little cab, with memories for company, as condensation obscured the outside world, and the air inside began to cool. On a normal day she would have been making dinner, reading the news, or settling down with a glass of wine, but here she wanted nothing more than time, and silence in which to welcome the past. She felt Jim step to one side, open the door to the Pump Room, saw him in the Cathedral, danced with him in Jane Austen's footsteps. They walked the Royal Crescent, admiring the curve and the view, rushed past the river and market in the autumn rain, stopped to buy cakes and eat them in Queen Square in spring. Bath was alive and Miss Bunne felt at peace.

Which was why, when a policeman tapped on the window, she jolted in her seat, before remembering where she was, and more worryingly, why.

"Madam, can I ask you what you're doing here?"

"Excuse me, why?"

"You're parked in a resident's bay, but you aren't displaying a permit. Also, your back tyre is slightly bald."

Miss Bunne wondered how such a well-maintained car could have a worn tyre but now was not the best time to get sidelined by her thoughts.

"Madam? Can I check your details please?"

"Yes, of course. I don't have any documents on me though, I wasn't planning on coming out tonight."

"Are you from around here?"

Miss Bunne suspected he was noting the car's registration.

"No."

"Then can I ask what's brought you here?"

Eileen Bunne felt alone with the danger in her situation. Not being used to deceit, she had no great ability to lie.

"I can't say, really," she managed.

"You can't say? And why is that? Have you had anything to drink tonight?"

Again, she managed a solitary, "No."

"I'm afraid I'm going to have to ask you to breathe into this tube, Madam. It's just routine. Please step out of the car."

He held out a breathalyser and as she stood in the cold street and blew into it, she was confident that at least that much would be clear. It was then he reached for his radio and spoke the damning words:

"Vehicle and driver check, please. Morris Minor, registration BRK 33..."

*****

A strip light is glaring and buzzing, most of the young men have been called but Miss Bunne remains straight backed, ankles crossed, handbag still on her lap. The heavy door opens, an usher runs his finger down the clipboard and, weary with waiting, she glances at her watch. He calls, "Miss Eileen Bunne." She stands, smooths her suit, and follows him down the long, wood-panelled corridor, past the vending machines and up the uncarpeted stairs, the signs for Court 1, 2, 3. As he opens the door to Court 4 and gestures for her to go in first, she straightens her spine, takes a deep breath, and walks toward the dock.

12

The Tempest of the Thames
by Vivien Eden

In that blest moment from his oozy bed
Old father Thames advanc'd his rev'rend head;
His tresses drop'd with dews, and o'er the stream
His shining horns diffus'd a golden gleam;
Grav'd on his urn appear'd the moon, that guides
His swelling waters, and alternate tides;
The figur'd streams in waves of silver roll'd,
And on their banks Augusta rose in gold.

Extract from Windsor Forest by Alexander Pope, 1713

December 23rd

The sky above me is currently a large knobbly blanket of pale grey and white with one, no two, small patches of blue. Just enough blue in the sky to patch a sailor's trousers as my mother-in-law would say. But we'd better stitch quickly because I can see some ominous looking clouds coming over from the east. More rain is expected. That's what has been keeping the temperature from plummeting; it really is surprisingly warm when I step outside. Eighteen degrees the outside thermometer says today. It makes the thought of receiving a hand-knitted jumper from my mum in a couple of days a little uncomfortable.

Christmas used to be colder, I'm sure. When I was about ten, I remember some remnants of snow on the ground one

Christmas morning. I remember it because my dad told me it wasn't a great idea to try my new bike out that day. "No Anton. You'll be slippin' all over the place, man," he told me in his big booming Caribbean voice.

My dad's from Grenada and came over here with his brother, for greater opportunities than their island could offer. They settled in West Croydon where an uncle kept an eye on them. When he was twenty-one, he met my mum at some party in Reading where he was tagging along. He tells me about the turquoise dress she was wearing that reflected in her ashen eyes giving them an ethereal glow – bewitching him. I'm not surprised, she is stunningly blond and pale. Dad jokes that she's see-through. She just tells him he's bloody gorgeous. I'll give him his dues; he looks pretty good for a sixty-year-old.

When Dad landed a catering job in Windsor the following year, he thought he'd hit the big time. Windsor's difference to Croydon was clear: more money, cleaner, safer… posher. Mum was happy to say goodbye to her insipid Reading family home for a new adventure with her man. Their wide eyes and young passion were in overdrive, and it was only a matter of weeks before mum fell pregnant with me.

So now, here I am, aged thirty-nine, living in Windsor: a mixed-race man. And I find myself part of a noticeable minority in this decidedly 'white' town. It's not usually a problem. Sometimes though, I just need to get out of here and go to places that are a bit more representative of what the real world is like. Take rugby. I love playing rugby. I have a strong, athletic build and I'm quick. I love the camaraderie, the rules, and the respect. Plus, tackling guys that are bigger than me gets out my aggression and makes me feel slightly better about myself. There's a perfectly good rugby club here in Windsor, but I prefer to drive half an hour to Uxbridge to play with a more ethnically diverse bunch of guys. Plus, I usually manage to persuade some of them to go to this great Caribbean restaurant over there for a little curry goat indulgence after training.

To earn my wage packet, I work for the Environment Agency. Although I'm a civil servant, I don't do it for the pension like some of my colleagues. I simply love nature and care about where I live. No crusty mates. No activist tendencies.

Lots of my time's spent outdoors, in particular along the Thames around Windsor and the Jubilee River. The team I'm in has a slightly oxymoronic sounding name – 'River Maintenance and Emergency Response'. Our job is to reduce the risk of flooding in communities and tackle waterway pollution. It's a good steady job and I even get to play the hero now and again when we get incidents. Like a 'water doctor' on call, I have to drop everything and go. It could be anything – the last one was a cow falling into the river.

How anyone could work for something like a 'tech' firm is beyond me: hot desking and sipping flat whites all day. I can see the difference I make when I work – the clear water, the constant speed at which it flows, the fish population thriving within it and my recent favourite – a new family of water voles. Now that's satisfying.

Moments of joy are important because often everything seems so dark. I need my water voles to cling onto. Lifebuoys, keeping me sane. The events that have made up my life don't really make sense when I think about them these days. It's as if parts were taken from someone else's life, someone happy and carefree.

I had a different life four months ago. A wife and two daughters, Megan who's eight and Freya – two years' her junior. We all lived together in our three-bedroomed house on the outskirts of Windsor, just off Hatch Lane. We had love and we had laughter. Sunday lunch at the dining table, bedtime stories and cuddles.

And then my head wasn't in that house anymore. Unbeknownst to me, I'd pushed everyone away. My wife was cold, or was that me? The girls started to treat me warily, like a stranger. The huge dark cloud came, and I couldn't get it to budge. I fixated on myself and how bad I was feeling, forgetting all about 'us'. My wife, Roxanne, she tried to help. Suggested I see someone, but I refused. Looking back on it, it was a combination of pride and my state of mind that caused me to make that decision. My alternative, far more basic, solution was to walk away before I infected them with my misery too. I even, quite ridiculously, hoped that a change of scene might help sort my head out… fat chance.

I know, I really dumped Roxanne in it. Bless her. Just before I left, I asked her mum if she could come and stay to help out with the kids. It was a rare example of me thinking of someone else.

More recently, I've had some long chats with my wife, who genuinely seems to want to know how I'm doing and continues to try and heal me. That woman never ceases to amaze me with the humanity and benevolence she displays – that's probably why she's so suited to nursing. One thing's for sure, the last thing she needs when returning from a long demanding shift is having to deal with my childlike behaviour as I wallow in self-pity. She deserves better than that.

That cloud still encircles my life: an amorphous nimbostratus with no beginning and no end. It suffocates and stifles. I hope it dissipates one day, but I can't imagine it will. For now, I'm still able to muster up a smile every Sunday when I see my girls. As they run towards me, my heart does this internal flip. Another lifebuoy. And then we go to McDonald's. Jesus.

It's two days before Christmas and I'm thinking of reasons to stay at work for as long as possible. I don't want to go back to my poky flat. I hate it. And yet I chose it.

December 24th

It's raining again. I'm over at the Jubilee River today. I like it here and often look for excuses to come over. Just before it was finished in 2002 it was eleven kilometres of intense eyesore. But now the reeds, trees and meadows are established, it's become a wildlife haven. Nature and bird experts ensured the plants, shrubs and trees would attract the right kind of flora and fauna to the area. We humans often do our best to destroy habitats in favour of our own. But the waterway here helps both man and beast. And it's so peaceful. Especially on a warm, rainy Christmas Eve.

Don't be fooled by appearances though. This place should only be enjoyed from its banks. Despite its calm-looking beauty, you wouldn't believe the ferocity of what the water is doing beneath the surface. Strong currents are *everywhere* and that's magnified around the weirs. Add to that that the sides are so steep you'll struggle to ever get out. Too many people have lost their lives in it. I've been called all sorts on a hot summer's day by lads in swimming trunks when I send them packing. But at the end of the day, it's a flood relief channel– not a swimming pool.

The Jubilee River twists and turns its way carrying river water along its length from above Maidenhead through Datchet. Some say that whilst it's done a fantastic job of alleviating flooding in Maidenhead, Windsor, and Eton, it's made the problem worse downstream. I don't really know if that's true. Independent studies refute this, but we'd possibly be better off asking the residents of Datchet and Old Windsor what they think.

Parking in my usual spot at the Marsh Lane car park between Taplow and Dorney, I notice a heron majestically ascending into the sky. A car park with a view, and also handily near one of my official hangouts: a water control structure which monitors and controls the water level.

Just a little walk downstream, within fifteen metres of the water, is my little secret though. Hardly anyone knows it's there. Due to the way the trees have been planted you have to stop midway between a purple willow and a hawthorn bush and turn your head sharply. Then you'll see two unpainted gate posts and a short gravel path. Look up the path and there it is – a little old, detached cottage poking out of some shrubs. All on its own.

It's been here far longer than the Jubilee River and belongs to the Crown Estate – nothing to do with the waterway at all. Originally it housed wardens who were responsible then, as now, for patrolling Windsor Great Park to keep it clean and safe. Unlike the well-known pink Crown Estate properties, this house is a stately pale green. It's flaking a little at the edges, but that's part of its charm along with the wild-flower garden, undulating roof and creaky lion-head door knocker. Climbing roses around the front door ensure it is chocolate box perfection.

There's a lovely lady called Jenny who lives there now with her nephew, Ollie. I've got to know them over the years I've been working here. Bit of a sad story really. Ollie's mum and dad were off the rails. Used to leave him alone as a baby overnight while they were out getting high. Social services got wind of it, so he now lives with his Aunty Jenny who is the most responsible person I know: she restores the royal art collection. I mean, The Queen wouldn't give all that expensive stuff to someone who wasn't completely trustworthy now, would she? Jenny's currently seeing some local cameraman chap - good luck to her, she deserves some happiness.

Ollie's now fifteen. Fantastic kid. Likes his computer games but is also really interested in the (feathered) birds round here, of which there are plenty, including woodpeckers, skylarks, storks, and warblers. I'll never forget the first time I met him and Jenny. Ollie was holding a blue feather he'd found on the path and was excitedly telling Jenny exactly what bird and which part of its body it was from. I've never seen such enthusiasm! We got chatting about what my job was and what bird species I knew. Now, when he spots me, he always offers me a cup of tea; sometimes, joining me on my patrols with his binoculars. And on those days, that human interaction helps to momentarily pick me up out of my melancholy. Lifebuoy.

Due to this relentless rain, the water seems to be moving faster than usual. If you imagine your average white van filled with water, that's the amount of water that usually flows through here per second. I'd say we're at about a 'single decker bus' flow today.

There's been some algae build-up on the water too. I need to keep an eye on that. Oh, and more plastic crap caught in the reeds. Thankfully I have my extra-long litter picker and permanent bin bag attached to my waist. Cola bottle, crisp packet, six-pack ring, sweet wrapper, bottle of water still with half the water in … is that 'bingo' yet? I chip away at the never-ending task.

At least I'm seeing the rugby boys tonight. Taxi to and from Uxbridge already booked for our Christmas party so that I can drink enough alcohol just to forget...

25th December Pre-turkey

I feel like death, but I think I look remarkably fine considering. Matty's idea of tequila shots at midnight wasn't the best plan. We tried to stop him, but he wasn't having any of it. In a flash, he was back with a wooden tray that looked like a ski holding eight shot glasses of the potent clear liquid. I was tempted to chuck mine in a plant pot, but they'd only make me do some horrible forfeit if they saw, so I just necked it. It was a bonding experience I suppose and at least I made it home without throwing up in the taxi, unlike one fella.

I've finished wrapping the last two presents for my girls and am good to go. I'd better walk round, considering the magnitude of my hangover, it'll help blow the cobwebs away. It's currently dry, but muggy, so I'll walk quickly before the inevitable cloudburst happens. Roxanne has asked that I stay for lunch and Mum and Dad are popping in too, which will be the icing on my Christmas cake, as it were.

*****

"There they are – my two little Christmas angels!"

"Daddy! Freya got one more present in her stocking than me, but mummy says I'm wrong, but I counted them. I don't think that's fair, do you?" comes the strangest Christmas greeting from Megan.

"Have you got us presents in that big plastic bag?" adds Freya. Why are children so materialistic?

"Do you think I could have a hug from each of you and then actually come in from this doorstep?"

Megan and Freya almost knock me over when they run and jump up on me. There'll be a women's rugby team wanting them in a few years.

"Girls. Come through into the lounge and have a play with your new toys," comes my wife's silken voice from inside the house. "Hi Anton, Happy Christmas," she leans over to peck me on the cheek… but it's Christmas… so sod it. I intercept her by gently cupping my hands either side of her face. She stops and looks into my eyes. Then, sensing that I'm not going to be slapped, I slowly pull her towards me, lessening the gap between us until our lips touch. We have a slow and sensuous Christmas kiss. I tingle throughout my body. She eventually

151

pulls away looking slightly bewildered, but not unhappy. "I see someone had a few drinks last night," she responds coyly. She turns away. "I've just made some coffee; would you like some or would you like to wait until your mum and dad get here in a few minutes?"

"I'd love one now please, Roxanne, I think I'll be needing a few this morning."

I follow her into the kitchen and find myself telling her that I've missed her. I'm slightly bewildered by this 'Christmas' version of me who snogs his wife impulsively and reveals his feelings –I must still be drunk.

"We've missed you too, Anton. Let's not be getting too deep and meaningful today though, hey? I've worked hard to get everything ready so let's just have some fun. Everyone's here together so no one should be missing anyone. Carpe Diem and all that."

And she's right. But I find my eyes welling up as I take in the scene. My wife's earnest face looking at me, overwhelmed by the tasks of the day ahead. My children through the open door playing and laughing. Why the hell have I abandoned them for all this time? I shut my eyes, it's too late, a tear starts to roll down my cheek. I feel a hand touch my shoulder. She knows me too well.

"Anton. Listen. I don't blame you for moving out, not for being prickly, not for all your sadness, your frustrations… You haven't been able to think clearly. You're ill, my love."

And there it is.

I sniff.

"And I'm so pleased you're starting to open up about your feelings a tiny bit, do you know why? Because that's how you'll get through this. By breaking down that wall you've built and letting those you love in. We all want to help you get better. Okay?"

I nod. And it is my most sincere nod ever.

"But it's Christmas and a day for celebrating." She moves behind me, pressing her body against my back and resting her chin on my shoulder. She turns her mouth towards my ear and says quietly, "Hey, you never know… if you want to have a few drinks today, you could always have a… Christmas sleepover." Her hand slides suggestively down my arm. "After a kiss like that and a few of your dad's festive cocktails later, there's no way of
telling what I might let you do to me if you play your cards right."

Clearly there is a 'Christmas' version of Roxanne that I had forgotten about. I rather like it.

"Oh no, what's the time now?" she starts.

"Five past nine"

"Time to get that Turkey in the oven."

December 25th Post-Turkey

As I sit nodding off on the sofa in my post-Christmas dinner haze, I feel an uncomfortable sensation around my groin. My phone is vibrating. Why, Lord, can I just not be left alone today?

Against my better judgement, I look at the screen. It's a text. From work.

<RED LEVEL WARNING. MALFUNCTION DURING PROCESSING. OPERATION 17 MARSH LANE IMMEDIATELY>

Having never actually seen one of these before, I can't remember what it's supposed to mean. I want to ignore it. Just then my phone rings. It's Larry, my line manager.

"Anton, Happy Christmas!" He sounds significantly more inebriated than me. I only had one glass of wine in the end due to my outstanding hangover.

"Happy Christmas, Larry. Is this anything to do with the alert that's just come through on my phone?"

"Yes, indeed it is. Are you pissed right now... because I am?!" Every fibre in my body is telling me to say that I am because I know what's coming.

"Not exactly, boss."

"Anton, I'm really sorry to ask you to do this, but could you pop over to Marsh Lane and reset the system. You just need to turn off the power and then turn it on again. It's flipped out like this before and the automated system is just going to start disturbing everyone with these damn messages all through the night otherwise. It'll take five mins and then you can get back to your Christmas fun and games. What do you say?"

"Should I give the place the once over when I'm there to check everything's okay?"

"Great idea, Anton, I'm going to remember this at your next performance review. Top man."

With heavy legs, I haul myself off the sofa and tell Roxanne and the girls I've got to go out for a quick work thing. She's not happy but tells me to be careful and to grab my spare waterproof coat from the cupboard because it's chucking it down.

I grab the coat, zipping it securely around me and head into the garage and find my old bike and helmet. My damn waterproof trousers are in the boot of my car, back at the flat. How I wish I'd driven here... never mind. It should only take about twenty minutes on the bike if I really go for it.

*****

Any hangover I may have had has long gone. That was a very invigorating journey. I go to the key safe outside Marsh Lane and enter the code. Grabbing the key, I quickly open the door and get out of the rain. It's only small in here but I can stand up straight and it's dry. On one wall is the computer system with lots of buttons. I know this place like the back of my hand and can immediately see something is up. One of the emergency buttons is flashing persistently. I peer closer to read which one it is – it says WEIR CONTROL.

Following Larry's instructions, I turn off the power to the system. I wait a couple of minutes in the dark room before turning everything back on. I eagerly wait to see whether the light has stopped flashing… it hasn't. How did I know this wasn't going to be as straight forward as I was led to believe?

I put my hood up again and quickly head outside to see if I can see anything. The first thing I notice is the water level. It's high and moving terrifically fast. The noise it is creating is absurdly loud. I think I can actually see it starting to come over the top of the channel just upstream from where I'm standing. How is the sodding flood relief channel… flooding? I take two enormous deep, slow breaths to try and calm my rising panic then grab a torch from inside the door. I shine the beam of light into the water to see what's going on.

With this level of water careering down, all the weirs along the Jubilee River should have automatically fully opened to allow the extra to pass through. Immediately I see that the tilting gates down at the bottom of the water haven't moved; they are almost vertical when they should be fully flat on the bed to allow the maximum flow to pass through. That explains why the water is pooling onto the bank at an alarming rate – it's stuck. I see something unusual shimmering around the bottom of the mechanism. It's golden in colour. Could that be what's causing the problem?

Running back inside, I frantically press the weir button to see if it has any effect. It doesn't. I have no idea what to do so I get on my phone and call the team emergency number. It rings nine times and then thankfully someone answers it.

"Happy Christmas, how can I help you?"

Yes, it's Christmas… I'd forgotten for a moment there.

"Hi, this is Anton Green, I'm at the Marsh Lane control station. Something is up with the weir – it's not working properly. The water is rising and starting to flood."

"Ho, ho, ho!" I can hear the smile on his face. He doesn't believe me.

"Look me up on the system: Anton Green, employee number 74362 – I've just had a call from my boss, Larry Turner, to reset the system here… I've left my wife and kids on Christmas Day to come here in the pissing rain and I don't know what to do!" I find myself shouting.

"Ok Anton, I'm sorry. Listen, my name's Neil…can you explain exactly what's happening there?"

"I've never seen this much water here. The weir gates here aren't opening properly so the water can't escape and it's now flooding quicker than you can say Christmas pudding."

"Right, I'm sending out a message to all the Berkshire emergency response teams asking for immediate assistance. Let's hope they're not all drunk, asleep or in the middle of… goodness-knows-what.

"While we're waiting for responses, let me check the system to see if I can see anything that might help us work out what's going on," and then he goes quiet on the line.

"Neil, are you still there?"

"… Yes, sorry. The system was just being a bit slow. OK… firstly I can confirm that Jubilee's weirs have definitely been activated due to the water flow. And you're saying that you don't think the one by you is functioning correctly?"

"That's right, it's hardly moved at all," I reply.

"OK, hopefully the help I've requested can sort the issue there. Let me take a quick look, working my way up the river from you, to see if anything else has been reported. Oh, this is interesting, it says here that at 11:45 today we had a call from a farmer outside Pangbourne expressing concern that the river had burst its banks and flooded his sheep's field… I suppose that on its own wouldn't have raised too many concerns. So… hang on, a Dr Engleberry from Oxford University alerted us at 10:30 to tell us his testing equipment had just measured some concerning water speeds. He didn't give any further details. He probably had some posh party to dash off to…"

I'm starting to lose patience. I fidget.

"Let me see if anything has gone on upstream of Oxford." I hear frantic tapping of keys "Holy f-… the Farmoor reservoir is full to the brim! It must have been absorbing the extra water from all this rain and now it can't take any more, so it's all coming
downstream… towards you!"

I stamp my foot in disbelief that a calamity such as this was allowed to happen. Then I notice the splashing sound my foot makes on the floor. Water has begun coming in through the door. I freeze. Something else is niggling at me… what is it? Then it comes to me in a vivid, horrid reality.

"I'll call you back, I have to go!"

I run outside and along the bank, noticing that the water now reaches my ankles in places. In the fading daylight, it's disconcerting that the river has no visible edge so I keep as far away from it as I can. I reach the gap in the foliage and run up the path. Reaching the door, I grab the creaky knocker and bash with all my might whilst shouting, "Jenny! Ollie! It's Anton, you need to get out – there's a flood!" I swear I can see the water moving up the path behind me, relentlessly pursuing me like a lioness wanting to eat me.

No answer.

I run to the front window. The curtains are drawn but there's a light on. I bash on the window. No answer. I try the next window and there, through a gap at the bottom of the blind, I see Ollie in front of his games console completely absorbed with his headphones on. How very festive. I see no sign of

Jenny. I scream Ollie's name. He hears nothing. I think about breaking the window, but there's nothing to hand and all I can hear is the sound of water: the rain sheeting down and the thunderous river. Mother nature is taking over and if I don't get back to try and sort this I'm going to be swimming back.

I sprint back to the control building and run inside. My phone rings. It's Neil.

"Anton?"

"Yes." I pant so hard I can barely get the words out.

"Right, I've managed to get hold of two people who can help you, but they are about forty-five minutes away."

I peer through the door and watch my bike get carried off by the water faster than I could hope to catch it.

"Is that the quickest anyone can do?! I can't wait that long. This place is going to be completely submerged and there's a cottage here with someone inside who's in real danger."

"Unfortunately, no one from Slough or Windsor is responding… there honestly couldn't be a worse time to have Christmas Day."

Something hanging on the wall catches my eye. Suddenly, I know what I have to do.

"I'll have to fix it myself then," I find myself blurting out.

"Err, how do you propose doing that?"

Speaking slowly, I unveil my plan to Neil as I simultaneously formulate it in my mind. "I think there's something wrapped around the weir gates, they're jammed. The buttons here are doing nothing so I'll have to try and manually release the gates."

"You don't mean…"

"It's the only way I can think of."

"No! I cannot allow you to enter the water alone. And especially not in the kind of conditions you're describing to me."

I think of Ollie, probably terrified with water up to his knees now. I ask Neil to call the emergency services and send them to the cottage. Who knows how long they will take to arrive today though? But I'm here, and I can do something. I hang up.

There's always a couple of sets of scuba diving gear here. Sometimes we have to go down and check out the riverbed if there's, say, an accumulation of silt or stones. I grab the scuba gear off the wall and strip down to my pants. Pulling the wetsuit over my body, it releases a musty neoprene smell and just for a moment I'm back on a dive boat in Mauritius with my wife… I check the tank for air, put on a weight belt, slip my arms into the buoyancy control device and do a couple of test breaths with the regulator. All good. So, I put some fins on my feet and wade backwards towards the edge of the river grabbing a long length of rope and a knife off the shelf as I go.

I tie the rope securely to the railings outside and slowly uncoil it as I walk. The water is up to my knees and the force is incredible. I acknowledge that I am going against everything that is humanly sensible right now. Scuba diving alone. In December. In a fast-flooding river. Next to an active weir. I think of Ollie… then slip the mask over my eyes and lower myself into the water.

And I'm in an immediate battle to not lose hold of the rope as the water furiously tries to wash it from me. My hands already hurt like hell from trying to keep hold of it. The unrelenting current just beneath the surface isn't going to let me get far, so I release some air from my buoyancy jacket and slowly sink to the bottom. The pressure in my ears is horrible, but it's a little less fierce here and I'm able to tentatively crawl across the bottom. The magnified sound of my breathing focuses my attention.

I see the blurry outline of the sinister-looking gate mechanism to my left and use it as a guide, feeling my way towards where I think I saw the gold-coloured object. Visibility is virtually non-existent, everything is bubbles and brown water, so I run my fingers along the bed and try to feel for something with my free hand. Suddenly I grab hold of some slimy plastic. I put my face right up against it and can make out a yellow-gold length of the stuff. It looks industrial and strong, and it shouldn't be here. This piece of plastic has literally *ruined* my Christmas Day.

I grab the knife and slash it into pieces which I pull away one by one and tuck into my weight belt to dispose of later. Finally, I heave the last bit away from under the gates and feel it release. I hear groaning and creaking; it's an unnerving sound. Even though I can't really see anything, I know that the weir gates must now be starting to flatten down onto the bed, so I need to get out of here. I allow myself to drift a little downstream so I'm a safe distance away, I don't want to get trapped underneath them. *Stay calm, Anton, and follow the rope as quickly as you can*. Pulling one hand in front of the other, I drag myself along towards the side. Already I can feel the force change down here as the gates lower and allow more water through. It's now so brutal that I feel my cheeks wobbling but I've made it to the side. I add a few pulses of air into my jacket to start my short ascent to the surface.

Why am I not rising? My leg feels stuck. I think my left fin might be caught on something. I lean over and see if I can release it, but it's wedged tightly. OK. I'll just slip my foot out and get out of here. My bare foot feels vulnerable as it wriggles free. I sacrifice the trapped fin to the water gods. Sorry river, I've just added to your pollution woes.

What the hell was that?

My head! Something has brutally hit the back of it. Maybe a tree branch being carried in this crazy water. I don't think my eyes are working properly, I see Christmas lights everywhere and feel incredibly giddy. Everything is going dark. I hear my breath…and then I don't.

No matter because I quite like this feeling. Everything is calm.

And quiet.

And I'm free. Free of it all.

And then I feel something. Or maybe I don't.

*****

No, no stop – leave me. Get off.

I see two silhouetted faces coming into focus. It takes me a moment but then I recognise Jenny from the cottage with a man I don't know.

"Anton, Thank GOD!"

"What are you doing here…?" my voice is unrecognisable as my own. Then I remember and try to scream "OLLIE!"

"Shhhhh," she says. "Ollie's fine." I notice I'm wrapped in a tartan blanket, but I'm shivering. The damp wetsuit feels disgusting against my skin. My brain feels foggy and I have a

huge pain in my chest.

"You are so lucky I spotted you, Anton."

"What happened?" I literally have no idea what is going on.

"Well, I was out having a quick Christmas drink at the pub with Dave here, my new fella."

"Hi there, mate," says the guy next to her, sheepishly. I notice his dark brown eyes. He has a kind face.

"Anyway, while we were there, I got a call from a very spooked Ollie saying that water was gushing into the house and that he didn't know what to do," she continued. "I told him to wait for us upstairs. So, we rushed back but by the time we arrived, very bizarrely, most of the water seemed to have…just gone. There were only a few puddles on the floor. Ollie was furious as his games console got wet and now won't work.

"I went outside to try and see what had just happened. That's when I found you over there entangled in some branches on the edge of the water, looking like Jacques Cousteau. You had all this gold plastic shimmering around your waist which is what I spotted first. Your face was a really horrible colour," her voice cracks a little. "I thought you were a goner, Anton. We managed to drag you out and call 999. They told us to do chest compressions and then water came out of your mouth – loads of it! And then you were breathing." She slouches a little; physically drained from reliving it.

I feel guilty that I've put her through that, but "Thank you," is all I manage to say.

"The ambulance should be here soon. We found your clothes and phone over in that building. Is there anyone you want us to call?"

I look up at the dark sky and realise it isn't raining anymore. Furthermore, the night feels crisp, like frost might even form. I stare at the immense black sky peppered with twinkling stars and notice one of them is unusually bright. Unblinkingly I watch it and notice how it moves slowly across the sky. Whether it's a satellite, a Christmas star or a jolly fat man on a sleigh is of no consequence. I see the beauty in it. And it is immense.

"Please can you call Roxanne, my wife," I reply, noticing flashing blue lights out of the corner of my eye.

"Absolutely no problem, Anton, what would you like me to tell her?" Jenny asks.

"That I'm coming home."

13
Christmas Concorde
By Phil Appleton

The four men had assembled in the side room of the coffee shop, glad of the friendly warmth of a packed café. Outside, as the Christmas Eve shoppers rushed, strolled and dawdled past on frosty pavements, the smokers accepted the enforced penance of their exclusion, in return for the comforting curls from their cigarettes. Inside, patrons queued patiently for their late morning treats as coffees, teas and soups were pushed across the counter, joining chocolate brownies, Danish pastries, and butter croissants on waiting trays. The beep of contactless cards punctuated the sound of happy, chattering voices filling the room.

It was Luke's turn to fetch the order, his three friends organising the stowing of hats, coats, and scarves, and keeping his seat. As an air traffic controller, he had automatically registered the overflying aircraft as he waited in line, confirming the easterly wind as the reason for the biting chill outside. All close to retirement, Luke, Mo, Nihal, and Matt looked forward to the end of their shift-working at Heathrow to spend more time together, and with their families. Arranging matching days off was always a challenge, with this day anticipated not only by themselves, but their wives too, happy to catch up in their own ways at church, mosque, gurdwara, and synagogue.

As Luke eased into his place, Mo reached eagerly for his tea, passing Nihal and Matthew their coffee en route. An airline engineer trained in Pakistan, Mo was excitable and expressive away from his work. He cupped his mug as he spoke, warming his hands.

"Did you see the International Space Station go over last night?" he asked. Luke sipped his coffee and replied, "Yes, like a star but fast moving and brighter. They've got a Russian, an American, and a Chinese man up there at the moment – I never thought that would happen."

Matt looked down at his plate, his thoughts at 60,000 feet.

"I remember the flight my wife and I took on Concorde for our thirtieth anniversary. We were on the edge of space seeing the curvature of the earth at twice the speed of sound – it was unforgettable."

"Yes," said Nihal. "I was on the day of its last scheduled flight into Heathrow – all eyes were on it – the most beautiful aircraft ever made."

"Well, everything's coming together for it to fly again," said Mo. "All the signs have told us it's the right time. We should get ready."

The four were members of The Believers, a worldwide inter-faith group, which also included contributors from the Sikh, and Buddhist population. Formed by travellers and explorers centuries ago, the modern network used the latest technology to bring together the best scholars of philosophy, science, and the arts. Those in the aviation industry had special responsibility for global communication. The mood of the men in the café had become pensive. Each stared at the table and became silent, immersed in their own private prayers. Then, as if choreographed, they stood up together, embraced, and left.

*****

At the same time, a woman in a black shawl was attending a confessional in her home village of Sainte Exupéry, Normandy. Marie Sainte-Agnès was a strikingly beautiful dark-haired woman of forty-five, taller than most French women, demure yet strong. Whispering to the unseen priest through the screen, she was nervous but unafraid.

"He has gone, Father. He should be in England by now. How should I pray?"

"You need not pray for him, my child," replied the priest softly. "He will be safe."

"He is but ten, Father."

"God is with him, my child. Pray for yourself, that you should remain patient and pure in thought."

"Yes, Father. Thank you."

Marie returned to her house, sparse yet comfortable, with flowers in a blue and white pottery vase on a dark oak cabinet reminding her of those she had carefully placed that week on the graves of her adoring parents, both long dead. Out of habit she checked the converted stable annex for tidiness; the place where her only son had been delivered, attended by the midwife, a shepherd, and Marie's faithful black Labrador. Unexpectedly that night, the Mayor, the Prefect, and the Chairman of the Departmental Council had come by to pay their respects and offer support.

An only child, Marie worked as a nurse and teacher to the younger children of the village. Books on cultures, religions, and politics from faraway places she had never visited spanned most of the walls of her home. Marie had been teaching herself English, after the visit from the stranger, which had opened a new dimension to her studies of ancient texts. Even though she wore the shawl of a married woman, no one asked about her husband or gossiped about her morals. Looked up to by her neighbours for her generous heart and gentle wisdom, she loved them all.

*****

One hour later, as the bells of Windsor Parish Church struck twelve noon, Marie's son stood up from his seat at the front of the train pulling into Riverside station. With lighter hair than his mother's, cut neat and short, yet with her smooth skin, he had an assurance in his manner that belied his age. His long, straight legs took him to the exit barrier, his green eyes looking up respectfully at the station agent as he inserted his ticket and passed through.

With a small backpack settled comfortably on his shoulders, the boy walked out into the sunshine and headed for Thames Street and the Theatre Royal. Glancing up to the castle he moved with gentle pace, unhurried and confident. He saw eager faces of tourists from every continent, local people with their children and dogs, and the occasional policeman or woman. As he climbed the hill, the scene unfolded up to Castle Hill, then left to right across the cobbles of Church Street and Market Street, a distant view of the Guildhall, to the Queen Victoria statue.

With his only knowledge of the outside world gleaned from books, the nuns at his school and his beloved mother, he marvelled at the sights. Slowing to a stop and resting his pack on one of the wooden seats backing onto the castle, he sat down and took a sip of water from his flask, drawn from the pump in his garden. He thought of his mother, caring and kind if a little anxious at times but devoted to him and the small community
in which he was raised. A happy and self-sufficient child wherever he was, the boy looked up at the sky and felt its connection to his home.

There, sitting in her armchair Marie felt apprehensive. She missed the comforting presence of her son, so calm and thoughtful despite his tender years. Yet Marie's faith in him and her God was strong, transcending any description of it in either

French or English. While some would reel off strings of Hail Marys and creeds to atone for their sins, she remained devout in her belief that 'God' was a benign presence constantly with her, reflected in the esteem and awe in which she was held by all around her. The only others who came close to her in grace and purity were The Believers, with whom she communicated on a daily basis. It was they who had told her when the stranger would be in Windsor, and to whose side the
boy would be unerringly guided.

While she knew she could count on her friends and neighbours for anything, she often thought back to the night of the storm and wondered if the man remembered her. He seemed so sure of himself in worldly matters, while she sensed a vulnerability that needed the kindness only she could bring. Now that she was alone, she thought of him with affection, wondering what had become of him after his departure from her home. While Christmas was always the highlight of the year in Sainte Exupéry, the memory of that Easter night had always stayed with her and been shared only with God.

Ten years on, Christmas week saw home-made gifts of food, hand-carved wooden toys, and knitted winter wear being exchanged in family gatherings in the village church, with children allowed to play in the aisles before and after daily Mass. This year, Marie had made them all warm gloves as gifts from Le Père Noël, Father Christmas in French. The sermon on Christmas Eve was always full of hope and expectation, while on Christmas Day it was all about joy and celebration. This year had been prophesied as exceptionally happy.

It had been the boy's unease at the myth of Saint Nicholas and all the other worldly incarnations of a man descending to earth with a bagful of presents that had finally impelled him to leave for England. His mother refused to believe in the Santa Claus story yet seemed curiously fixated by Le Père Noël, and also the English language and the similarities between it and her own. For his part, her son had always been drawn to Windsor, colonised by his ancestors the Normans who had built the magnificent castle behind him a thousand years before.

Now the streets were full of cars, vans, bicycles, and the occasional noisy motorbike. Except for one – Peascod Street, falling away to the south with only pedestrians filling its space below the glittering Christmas lights hanging overhead. The boy's scan continued right past a bank, hesitating for an instant at the bus shelter then on down the hill following a sweeping curve of shops and restaurants, before returning to the glass of the shelter where he had sensed rather than seen the object of his visit to the town. The boy crossed Thames Street near the entrance to the Royal Shopping Centre with the sellers of cheap souvenirs at their stalls, ignoring their temptations. Neither he nor his mother had time for trinkets.

*****

The man was unkempt and clutched a can of beer. A purple carrier bag and a canvas holdall lay next to his cardboard bed and sleeping bag, with a plastic box within his reach. He was wearing a thick Russian-style overcoat, a knitted scarf and woolly hat. Tanned and weather-beaten, his skin colour offset a thick growth of white beard, under bloodshot but still sparkling blue eyes. His manner vigilant and alert, he looked up as the boy approached and smiled as the lad met his gaze and tossed some coins into the box, more than he expected.

"Hello." said the man.

"Good afternoon." replied the boy.

"You have a slight accent. Where are you from?"

"France. And you?"

This was unusual. Tourists never normally asked questions.

"Here. I live here."

"What is your name?"

"Joseph, but you can call me Joe. What's your name? And where are your parents?"

"Noël. I came to find you."

"What do you mean, "you came to find me?""

"You just have to believe."

"What, in Father Christmas? Yeah. Right, handing out presents that nobody wants? Twenty years of flying and that's what I've come down to, being seen as bloody Father Christmas dressed up in this stupid outfit." Joe gestured towards the carrier bag exposing a scarlet tunic with white rings on its arms.

"You were a pilot," said Noël.

"Yes. I had to stop because of an incident – and I won't be Father Christmas much longer either, because they've got a woman doing it now."

Noël waited patiently for more, then continued.

"I have some gifts to deliver. Will you help me?"

Joe looked intently at Noël. As part of his employment, he had been checked as safe to work with children but was still wary of the risks of being seen talking to them alone. Yet he felt at ease with this one. He had learnt to trust his instincts, and now he felt compelled to follow the boy's lead, out of character for a pilot with ten thousand hours flying time in command. He nodded.

"Okay. How long will it take? I'll need to pack up my bed."

"Leave it. Come as you are. You are a pilot now."

"No. They took my licence away after the crash."

"You're going to fly again."

Joe wondered how much he had had to drink. He looked at the beer can for clues, 4.8% alcohol by volume. That looked real, but he wasn't so sure about the boy standing in front of him.

"Who are you?" he asked.

"I'm Noël."

"So you said. But who are you?"

Before Noël could respond, a passer-by moved between them to drop a coin in the box, breaking the moment. Joe took a final sip of beer, set down the can and stood up, scooping up all the cash and stretching his aching body. Perhaps he had drunk more than he thought, he certainly felt relaxed. He'd lost his money from the previous day at the betting shop, so was grateful for what the boy had given him. The least he could do was help him deliver a few presents. Besides, he had nowhere else to go.

"I need to freshen up round the corner, and then get some food. Will you look after my things for me?"

"Yes. I have food. No more beer."

Glaring at Noël, Joe felt anger rising in his chest. Who was this kid telling him what to do? Then, inexplicably his eyes lowered, and he felt a sudden peace fall over him. There was stillness in the boy's demeanour that was both unsettling and reassuring. Joe walked calmly and quietly away towards the public toilets in the precinct.

Noël sat down on the cardboard and bit into the croissant that his mother had packed, followed by an apple from the tree she tended. There was more but his mother had taught him to pace himself and appreciate his food. She had thought hard about letting him go on his own, but The Believers had assured her that he would be looked after. Part of the same following, the priest and elders of Sainte Exupéry's congregation confirmed this too – they had all shared and read the same texts.

Most people who had heard of Nostradamus thought he only prophesied disasters and calamities, but those who had access to the Seer's original sixteenth-century manuscripts knew otherwise. Hidden in a secret vault in the nearby town of Bécherel, the foretelling of the greatest world event since the first Christmas was revealed only to The Believers. After the birth of her child, Marie had been allowed unrestricted reading of the texts, trembling with anticipation as her premonitions had been confirmed.

*****

Having washed and shaved, Joe returned carrying a supermarket bag and, once he had laid it down, stared at the plastic box. It was full of banknotes and coins, to a value of well over a hundred pounds, more than he had ever made in a week on the streets. He looked hard at Noël, watching as the boy raised himself in one easy movement. Joe was a tall man, who carried himself upright and with dignity, but for one fleeting second he imagined Noël was taller. He found himself feeling uncomfortable in a way he had never experienced before, in awe of his young companion.

"So, what's the plan?" he asked quietly.

"The car is here," replied Noël.

Matt, a customer service agent all his working life, had parked his people-carrier in the lay-by and was waiting ready with   a rear door open. Joe removed his coat to reveal a torn and tattered uniform jacket with four captain's rings and took his place   on the back seat. Noël sat next to him, they all strapped up and Matt set off towards Sheet Street and the A308 to Staines and Heathrow. Crossing the Long Walk, Joe and Noël listened to Matt's briefing.

"They're loading the last of the presents now," said Matt. "With the Internet and online shopping there aren't many people who believe in Father Christmas anymore, but we've still got enough to fill the plane."

"Which languages are the books printed in?" asked Noël.

"They're just in English. Other countries are doing their own thing. It's not like in the old days, when we had a whole fleet of aeroplanes out."

"It's time for people to reassess their lives. The last lockdown was part of that."

"Yes, to think people actually believed you could deliver thousands of presents in a flying sled pulled by reindeer!"

*****

To the east, The Believers were busy at Heathrow's engineering base preparing the Concorde for departure: checking the fuel and systems, removing the engine covers, and stripping the cabin of seats to accept a full load of freight. The tyres had been pumped up to their take-off pressure, the onboard computers had been booted up, and Luke had entered the flight plan into the air traffic control system. Mo looked on with satisfaction as the 185 tonnes of sleek, white metal was towed into position by a tractor. Matt drove his car to within a hundred metres of where the plane had been stopped. Noël turned to Joe.

"Ready?" he asked.

"I haven't flown for years, and I've certainly never flown anything like this," replied Joe.

"Trust me. I trust you."

Noël and Matt got out of the car, Matt moving away to speak to Nihal who was supervising his team of loaders, while Noël went round to the back of the car to collect Joe's holdall, leaving Joe time for his private thoughts. Joe was wondering if he had gone mad, many homeless people were labelled as mentally ill. The accident hadn't been his fault; the storm had been one of the worst in history. The downdraft from the thundercloud had thrown his freighter out of the blackness of the sky into a field, and then it had skidded into the trees

173

smashing windshield, wings, and engines. Perhaps his brain had been damaged too.

He remembered the dazed walk to a house, the torrential rain, and the vision of the woman - surely a fantasy, a malfunction of his mind after the stress of the impact. He had an almost brain-dead journey back to Windsor, and then a zombie-like existence on its streets with drink and gambling for company. Until now, on another dark night but this time with moonlit brightness, friendly faces all around and the mysterious Noël, seemingly the centre of attention, but unaffected by it all. Joe stared at Noël, seeing only kindness, empathy, and patience in the lad. He got out of the car to join him, his few belongings left behind, forgotten as evidence of his past life. It was time to fly. He looked up at the steps leading to the aircraft door and turned to Noël.

"Who are you?" he repeated.

"Just believe in me, as I believe in you. Go on up."

Noël followed Joe up to the cockpit of the gleaming Concorde, taking the empty right-hand seat. Mo appeared at the doorway.

"Joe, we're all set with just over twelve tonnes of payload on board, and fuelling is complete. God is most great."

"Okay, Mo, thanks. See you whenever." It was as if sitting in a supersonic airliner loaded with Christmas presents was the most obvious thing in the world.

*****

In Sainte Exupéry, Marie put more logs on the fire in her cosy living room and returned to the kitchen where she had soup simmering on the stove, and a cake baking in the oven. The night was quiet and peaceful, in contrast to the violent storm that had struck the village and its surrounds a decade previously and caused her to fear for her life. She could still hear in her mind the screaming and roaring sounds across the sky from the stricken plane, which had rocked the house to its foundations. Then the stirring of her dog before the stranger knocked on her door in the pouring rain, exhausted and bedraggled, looking for a place to stay.

With a wagging tail, the dog had immediately approached the man, giving Marie the signal to trust and care for him. She had brought him towels; fed him, and given him a bed, all in silence as neither spoke each other's language. Shaken by the crash and his battle to get his aircraft down safely he had appeared vacant and oblivious to her, while he was wondering if he had died and was in the presence of an angel. The dog had watched over him during the night ready to protect Marie, but as the storm subsided and sleep overtook them all, only a profound peace existed in the house, remaining until the stranger left the next day.

✶✶✶✶✶

Working through a checklist again gave Joe renewed confidence, as he completed the engine start sequence, watching with satisfaction as the temperature and oil pressure readings on the four mighty turbojets reached their green levels. He checked Noël's and his own straps and harnesses. He was surprised and pleased that the lad had quickly found and put on the headset provided.

"Heathrow Ground, Concorde ready for departure."

"Roger Concorde, runway 27-Right, wind calm."

It was a woman's voice, clear and reassuring.

"You are cleared for take-off at your discretion, unrestricted climb and speed, own navigation as flight planned. Radio silence approved. Happy Christmas."

"Thanks. Leaving now and have a good one yourself."

"God bless you, Joe. Out."

Joe liked the caring sound of the woman's voice; it reminded him of the French woman whose soft tones had never left him, sustaining him as his life and career had disintegrated.

*****

As Marie sat down to eat, Joe pushed the throttles fully forward, kicking the afterburners into life and starting to accelerate down the two miles of Heathrow's tarmac. Outside, The Believers watched as Concorde lifted off in a shattering crescendo of crackling power with its fires of burning fuel, as others cursed the noise and disruption to their lives. With the undercarriage and nose visor raised, Joe engaged the autopilot, trusting the electronics to fly the most efficient track to deliver his cargo over London, then the rest of the United Kingdom. Rising up into the clear air, they turned the plane north over Windsor as the presents began to drop from its belly. Joe and Noël removed their headsets, looking out at the night sky.

"Beautiful sight. It's all coming back," said Joe.

"Let it, let go. This is your time," replied Noël.

Joe looked intently at him.

"You're a very unusual young man."

Noël smiled kindly.

"That's what my mother says."

"And your father?"

"Let's eat."

He reached into his bag for the remainder of his lunch, offering it to Joe: a baguette with salted butter, gruyère cheese and ham.

"That didn't come from Waitrose. Theirs is fine, and they sometimes let me have some of their left-overs, but I haven't had anything really fresh in years."

"Take it. I'll have yours. There'll be more at home."

As the boy handed over his lunch, Joe saw the same gesture in him that the French woman had made when she gave him food all those years ago. His heart began to race, and he looked forward at the thousands of lights apparently crawling, but in reality moving towards them at hundreds of miles per hour. At their current speed, she was less than half an hour away. Joe spoke softly.

"Where did you say you were from?"

"Sainte Exupéry in Northern France."

"Antoine de Saint-Exupéry was a famous French aviator and writer."

"Yes."

"I had to divert to France once because of a storm. I crash landed in a field and ended up at someone's house. I don't remember anything after that."

"Right."

"I'm tired." said Joe, yawning. "Flying again is great, but I just want some peace now."

He allowed his eyelids to close for a few seconds, then fell asleep as the autopilot steered them over Birmingham, Wales, then Northern Ireland and Scotland before arcing east and south back to London. As Joe slept and the night passed, Noël allowed himself to slip into a state of trance-like relaxation, with the comforting majesty of the heavens enveloping him like a blanket, in preparation for the day that was about to unfold. When Joe finally woke, Noël was calmly looking up at the stars and seeing the moonlight reflecting off the vapour trail of an overflying plane, high above them.

Joe pointed to a counter on the instrument panel that read zero.

"That's the payload delivered, so we can go home now. I'm ready."

The navigation systems took them east then into a right turn to follow the river down from the Thames Estuary towards

Windsor. A misty glow filtering up from the rising sun was signalling the breaking dawn.

"Are you not tired?" Joe asked Noël.

"No. I knew this day would come and I too am ready. It was written."

"What do you mean?"

"My mother learnt it from the texts. The priest and the nuns in my village confirmed it. The Believers have been preparing for this day for two thousand years."

Joe turned to the instruments, seeking normality in their steady readings; overwhelmed by what he was hearing, while accepting that he was in a new kind of reality that he couldn't begin to understand. Yet for the first time in his life he felt at one with himself and the world, and it was fun too. He would give the inhabitants of Windsor, and his homeless friends a show while he had the chance – a Christmas flypast down the Long Walk.

*****

A soft grey light was spreading as the Concorde flew over London, streets, cars and houses below them. As the autopilot locked onto the approach and landing radio beam, Joe and Noël heard Luke's deep Caribbean voice sequencing the morning traffic into Heathrow as they put on their headsets. The radio transmissions were sounding more intense, and Joe had to wait for an opportunity to speak.

"Concorde, Heathrow, back on frequency, on approach for 27-Left."

"Roger, Concorde. Good morning. You are cleared to land, wind two six zero at ten knots."

Joe glanced across at Noël, seeing Marie again in the boy's features, and for a second his own, feeling his heart swell with elation and energy. His head was telling him he had to land, yet something far more powerful was pulling him away.

"Let's wake everyone up," he said.

Pressing the autopilot disconnect switch, Joe turned left and called Luke.

"Concorde, initiating Christmas flypast over Windsor Castle."

"I can't authorise that, Joe." replied Luke, yet there was no concern in his voice. He and The Believers knew what was happening in the cockpit of Concorde and could see and hear it approaching.

"Passing Runnymede and maintaining one hundred feet. All good." said Joe.

"Roger, Concorde. Take care."

Joe turned the Concorde sharply right to level it down the centreline of the Long Walk. At two hundred miles per hour it would only take a minute to reach the castle. Its imposing outline began to fill the skyline, the Royal Standard fluttering gently in the breeze. Maybe the Queen was watching. The trees flashed past as early morning joggers looked up and covered their ears. With the aircraft thundering towards the castle gates Joe applied full power and gently pulled back on the control column, turning to Noël and smiling.

"Thanks, son," he said. "You have control."

Noël pressed the starboard radio transmission switch, as he had seen Joe do on his side.

"London, this is Concorde."

"Concorde, Joe?"

"This is Noël. I have control. I'm diverting to France to see my mother and drop my father off, then I'll be back, as you expected."

"Jesus," cried Luke, "is this really happening?"

"Only if you believe it." said Noël.

A Hundred Words

By Phil Appleton

Only one event could entice four hundred locals to a dark, wet, closed-off street late on a December Monday in Windsor. Rain or snow – the warmth of friendly greetings, scarves, and funny hats took care of either. Jacket potatoes, hot dog stalls, and two mulled wine tables added more heat and comfort, with bar staff in Santa outfits handing out sausage rolls and mince pies. The singing eventually graunched into life, becoming more random and out of tune. But none of those present cared – The Two Brewers carols was the start of Christmas for them – and few missed it.

14

A Haunted Christmas

By Rosa Carr

Three weeks to Christmas

From up here the world is right.

Standing at the top of the hill under the big horse statue, you can forget about everything. The only thing you need to worry about up here is the frosty grass, the occasional fellow runner, and the odd bike whizzing by.

Up here, there is a beautiful view down to the castle with only greenery in sight. There are no planes roaring overhead, no cars clogging the roads like arteries filled with cholesterol, no people jostling for the last items on the shelves.

Sighing, you accept reality and head back down.

You jog up to the big white fence with a slight sense of dread. You step through the gate which is meant to keep the deer inside but instead feels as though you're heading into captivity.

You cross the road, dodging traffic. Up the streets until you reach yours.

Outside your house, you pause for a moment, and take a deep breath. With no excuse to stay outside, you brace yourself, walk up the path and unlock the door.

Closing the door behind you, you look around the entryway. Nothing looks out of place. You take two steps forward and look into the lounge.

You sigh.

There in the middle of the room is a cardboard box. You've never seen this box in your life.

It has happened again.

Since you moved into this house in October, strange things have been happening. It started on Halloween night with the cats, the lights flickering, and what you tried to convince yourself was a fault in the wiring and the atmosphere of the evening, not... no, it wasn't possible!

Then you noticed things moving around. Nothing missing but things were adjusted as though you had chosen the wrong place for it.

Slowly, you walk up to the box. Keeping it at arms' length, you hook a finger under the flap. Turning your face away, you pull the flap up. Nothing jumps out so you take a closer look. Inside, is a jumble of -

"Christmas decorations?" you ask out loud.

The box has tinsel and fairy lights, even a few tree decorations. You look around to see where you can put everything.

Oh, I don't have a tree. Hang on! Where on earth did this box come from?

Walking out of the lounge, you go upstairs, then on a whim, you get the ladder and climb up to the loft.

There is another box with a tree up there and a patch free of dust where the other box sat. You grab the tree and slowly make your way back down.

Pulling out your phone, you find the number of the estate agent who sold you the house.

"Hi, this is Ella," you say and give your address.

"Oh, yes, hello. How can I help?"

"I found something in the loft, and I wondered whether you had the contacts for the previous owner?"

"Ah, well, let me see." You can hear computer keys clicking. "Right. I thought so. Ok. So, uh, Ella. Do you remember when you bought the house, I... uh... mentioned that the owner had died?"

"Oh no! I had forgotten! Quite young you said?"

"Yes, that's right. Was it something valuable? I could try to track the estate."

"No. It's just some Christmas decorations, but you know, sometimes they have sentimental value."

"I see. Probably best not to try to return them. Put them up? Or perhaps just throw the lot out if it's too weird?"

You say goodbye and disconnect.

Taking the tree into the living room, you don't unpack it. Feeling down from the conversation, you head to the kitchen and make some brunch: pancakes for comfort.

Once you've fried a stack, you decide to splurge a bit and get the syrup. It's up on the highest shelf, behind the flour — hasn't been used in ages.

Stretching up, your hip nudges the flour, and it tips over.

Damn!

A layer of white dust covers the counter. Sighing, you turn to get a cloth.

When you look back, your breath catches.

put up the tree!

You stare at the message written in the flour. You blink a few times, but the message is still there.

You get control of your shallow breaths.

Ok, just play along. You need a tree anyway.

You unpack the tree. Opening the other box, you pull out the fairy lights. You decide to test the lights before draping them around the tree.

Just as you thought: they don't work. Ok, so you'll need to buy new ones.

You take your coat and bag and leave the house.

Thankful for the escape, you walk into town but make a stop in a park.

Sitting on a bench, you pull out your phone; you're about to redial the estate agent but then pause. Instead, you open a browser and search for the obituaries from early in the year.

You read three before you realise how depressing it is. But you need answers. You keep scanning, looking at their ages. After about fifteen, you find one that fits:

Adam Shaw, 34.

He had lived in Windsor for a few years and died unexpectedly. He studied business and went on to have a successful career in the City. He studied at —

The same university as you!

He would have been finishing his degree the year you started yours. You don't recognise the name. But why would you? You didn't study business. And even if you had, you wouldn't have known the students in their third year.

To complete the stalking session, you search for his name and find a photo.

Your body goes cold, and you hear your blood pounding in your ears. Oh my God! The screen blacks out but you keep staring.

A clatter brings you back to your senses. Looking down, you see that your phone has fallen, but thankfully, it's unbroken.

Picking up your phone, you hurry into town. You vaguely notice Santa with a queue of children. You weave your way between the Saturday shoppers, made into a bigger mob by the upcoming festivities.

In a daze, you go to the hardware store and buy fairy lights.

On your way home, you pass two homeless people and feel a stab of guilt and fish around for some coins for them.

Now alone in your house, the house that belonged to – him! After all this time! – you fight back tears, you put up the tree and decorate it with the new lights and the old decorations.

Once that's done, you go to the kitchen, take a photo of the message. You're about to spread the flour out again but reconsider and gather the flour into a heap. Instead, you put out a notepad and pen. You leave the kitchen, thinking that the ghost may have stage fright.

Later that evening, you go back to the kitchen and look at the notepad.

The tree looks great!

The note is scrawled across the notepad as if written by a child, or someone using their non-dominant hand.

"Ah, you've upgraded from flour to pen and paper now? Cool," you mutter. Then you brush the leftover flour into the bin and turn to a clean page in the notepad.

Two weeks to Christmas

You haven't had any more messages from your ghost pal. The tree looks great in the corner. Hopefully he is at peace now.

Your phone rings.

"Hi, Mum."

"How are you, honey?"

"Fine. How's St Lucia?"

"Oh, it's lovely, dear. The beach is spectacular, I do wish you were here!"

"Yes, well, I just bought a house so it's not something I can splurge on right now."

"I know. But we do miss you!"

"I miss you too, Mum. How's Dad?"

"Oh, he's having the time of his life. He's snorkelling and whatnot."

"Great, Mum. Have you — sorry Mum, there's someone at the door. I'll call you later. Bye."

You put your phone down and hurry over to the door.

There's a man standing there.

"Hi?"

"Oh, hi!" The man's smile fades slightly as he tilts his head. "I should have called first. I'm here to see Adam."

"Oh." Crap! Doesn't he know? Who the hell is he?

"Adam's not here." You cringe at your awkwardness.

"I really should have called first. Will he be back soon?"

You frown. "He doesn't live here anymore."

"Shit! Being spontaneous is really biting me in the ass now. This was the last address I had for him. I didn't know that he moved. I'll call him now. Sorry to have bothered you." He turns to leave.

"Wait," you say. He half turns around. "Are you a friend of his?"

He turns back fully and looks at you. "Uh… yeah. It may not seem like it, but he's my best mate. I've been travelling for a few months, off the grid."

"How long?"

Now he's frowning. "About a year."

"I think you should come in." You don't know what comes over you. Why are you getting involved in this? It's not your business. But getting this news over the phone would be terrible. And if he ended up calling Adam's family? That would be devastating for them.

"No, it's ok, I'll just call Adam." His eyes are darting over you.

You sigh, out in the open it is then. "You can't call Adam. He's… um… he died."

The man's shoulders drop, and he looks like he's melting as he stumbles forward. You reach out instinctively and grab his arm. Gently you tug him into your house and guide him to the sofa.

"I didn't… I wasn't," he mumbles.

"I'll get you some water."

You head into the kitchen and glance at the notepad that you had left in place of the flour.

SORRY!

You shrug. Nothing to be done about it now. You grab a glass and fill it with water.

"Here."

"Thanks. I'm Jamie, by the way."

"I'm Ella."

"I've been away. I hadn't heard."

"I'm sorry. I bought the house in October. I found out that he died earlier this year."

You let him sit in silence for a few minutes.

"Last year has been quite rough. I work in banking and it's a very stressful job. Adam chose a job that doesn't suck you dry... I should have followed him. But I was young and wanted quick money. One day, I realised that I couldn't do it anymore. I quit my job and started backpacking around Asia. I came back now for a few months, then I was planning to go to South America."

"Wow," you say quietly.

"I was planning to visit Adam for a bit, and maybe see my sister and a few other mates. But it was mainly Adam that I came back to see because I hadn't heard from him..."

He drops his head into his hands, and you see his shoulders shake. You ease yourself off the sofa and head into the study.

You sit at your desk and scroll through your phone. A notepad catches your eye: it's out of place and —

Invite him to stay for Christmas.

"Seriously? You want me to invite a complete stranger to stay for Christmas? What, should I say that my ghost pal, who happens to be your dead friend, wants you to stay?"

shrugs

"Gee, thanks for the help! Are you going to talk to him?"

He underlines one word:

shrugs

You sigh and push the notepad away and roll your eyes. "Fine, I'll ask."

As you walk into the lounge, you see that Jamie is sitting drinking the water.

"Sorry you had to find out this way."

"Thanks. I've cut myself off from my old life for a while now, I've ignored many attempts at communication. I should have paid more attention."

"What are you going to do now? Go to friends or family?"

"Nah, except for Adam, all my friends are bad influences. I don't want to see them. And, well, things aren't great with my family. I... don't know. Guess I'll find an AirBnB or something for a couple of days while I organise flights somewhere."

You brace yourself and silently swear at your ghost pal. "You could stay here if you want."

He raises his eyebrows.

"My parents are away for the holidays. I can stay at their house, and you could stay here if you want. Until you figure out what to do. It might not be that easy to get last-minute flights now over the holiday period."

"You sure? Is their house far away?" He frowns.

"Yeah, I'm sure, it's fine. Nah, they live about 15 minutes' drive from here."

"Ok, if you're sure. I'll pay you, of course."

"No need. Just buy groceries or whatever."

He nods.

"And if you're up for it, I'm having Christmas Day lunch with a couple of friends."

"Yeah, maybe."

"I'll grab some things and then leave you to it."

You head upstairs, leave some clean sheets and towels in the spare bedroom, and then fill a bag.

"Here's my phone number and a key," you say. "I'll stop by tomorrow?"

"Sure. And thank you. This is very kind of you."
You nod and walk out the door.

*****

Later that night as you are sitting watching Netflix, you get a text message:

Hey. It's Jamie.
I saw a note in the kitchen that said 'tree topper'.
Can I join you?

You stare at the message for a moment. What is the ghost playing at?

Hey.
Yes of course.
I'll stop by tomorrow around eleven and we can wander around town.

Great!

Is everything ok? Have you found everything you need?

Yeah. All good thanks.
Just watching Netflix, hope you don't mind.

No worries!

*****

The next morning you drive over to your house. You put the key in the door and pause. You ring the doorbell and count to 5 before letting yourself in.

Jamie is walking towards the front door.

"Hey."

"Hi. You ok?"

"Yeah, great. Shall we go?"

They walk down the road together, chatting.

"Have you been here before?"

"Yes, ages ago. When…" Jamie clears his throat. "When Adam first bought the house. I visited him a lot. Did some of the touristy stuff," he says and points to the castle in the distance. "Have you lived here long?"

"Before I bought the house, I lived nearby. So, I've been relatively local most of my life."

You wander along Peascod Street, weaving in between the shoppers.

"Let's go further up and get away from the high street," you suggest.

You walk away from the castle. Once you're away from the hustle and bustle of the main shopping street, you start to notice smaller, less commercial stores.

You turn down a side street randomly and are stopped by a woman outside a shop.

"Oh, excuse me. Can you tell me how to get to," she pauses and looks down at a piece of paper, "Clarence Crescent?"

"Sure," you direct her and see her on her way.

As she walks away, you see the gift shop that she's just come out of.

"This looks good."

You walk in and after a lap around, you find the perfect Christmas tree topper.

Happily, you leave and suggest lunch.

*****

192

Later that afternoon, once you have dropped off Jamie and the shopping, you are sitting at your parents' house watching a movie, when your phone buzzes.

Hey. Would you mind coming back here?

Is everything ok?!

Yes, I just need to show you something.

You hurry to get your bag, cursing the ghost. Has Adam revealed himself to his friend?

When you arrive at your house, you don't pause to ring the doorbell this time but let yourself in.

Jamie is standing in the lounge looking ashen.

"Hey, what's going on?"

"I was thinking about getting some food. And I didn't want to bother you. So, I was looking for your address. I went into your study. I swear I wasn't snooping. And I found this."

He hands you your notepad and the top page has a message:

Hey JayGee. Miss you buddy.

"Um. So that's…"

"Adam? Yeah, I know. He's the only one who called me that. Gordon is my surname."

"Yeah, it's Adam. Shall we sit so I can explain?"

You tell him everything, from Halloween all the way to now. All the anomalies and strangeness around the house.

"And it was only recently that he actually started writing to me. At first it was in some flour that I spilled a couple of weeks ago."

"A couple of weeks ago? When exactly?"

"Um," you think back. "Saturday? Saturday before last? I think." You look at Jamie closely. "Why?"

"Ok, so on Monday, I went into the village and connected to my emails. I don't often check in. I saw an email from Adam inviting me over. It had been a while since I had seen him, so I decided to come. And then you told me…"

"This is insane!"

"Yeah, I know! When you told me, I thought that the email had gotten delayed in delivering. But then I saw this note."

"So, there's something else. One second."

You hurry into your study and find an envelope. Back in the lounge, you hand it over.

Jamie opens it and pulls out your degree certificate. He scans it then freezes.

"You went to—,"

"The same uni, yeah. I read Adam's obituary and realised. And I recognised him, I think."

"Really?"

"Yeah. Um, there was this guy in the library that I would see often. I never spoke to him, but I think it was Adam."

"No way! You're the library girl! What the actual fuck are the chances of that!"

"Oh…"

"He used to talk about you. Said that I should go with him and meet you. I dunno, he seemed to think you were my type."

You are speechless.

"I was going to. I mean, he went on about it so much that eventually I gave in. But then he broke his leg and couldn't manage to get around campus much. Then we finished and I forgot all about it. Bloody hell! Still playing matchmaker."

You both sit in silence for a while.

"I should probably leave. It's weird now?"

"Um, yeah a little. But you don't need to leave. It's Christmas

194

in a few days. Stay for Christmas lunch. I'll stay at my parents'
until then, give you some time."

*****

Two days later, your phone buzzes.

You've got ghostly mail.

Oh?

A picture arrives of the note:
What's Christmas without gifts?
£30 limit

You up for it?

Sure. I'll meet you on Peascod by M&S

It's crazy but the ghost, Adam, seems to have good
intentions and Jamie seems nice.

You meet Jamie outside M&S.

"Hey!" you say as you get closer.

"Hi. I'm glad you came."

"You didn't think that I would?"

"Yeah, as though I thought maybe this was some giant
scam," Jamie says, ruefully.

"Some trick that would be, to write notes without being
seen."

"Wait, you actually saw the notes being written?"

You look around, people are too absorbed in their own
minds and conversations.

"Yeah. When you had first arrived, Adam was convincing
me to ask you to stay."

"Damn! So, this is very real."

"You really thought that I was scamming you?"

He laughed. "It did cross my mind."

"Let's split up to get these presents, then meet up to have lunch?"

"Sure."

You watch him wander down the pedestrian-only road and you go into Daniel's, the department store next to M&S. You haven't bought anything for a man in a while but you're sure you'll find something suitable in here.

Christmas Day

You and Jamie are in your kitchen preparing a grand lunch. You chat away like you've known each other for years. You are also assisted by Adam who occasionally nudges ingredients closer to you.

You have told your friends that you have an extra guest and when they arrive, they are all clearly curious and pepper him with questions.

Over dessert, the question that you have been hoping won't come up is asked:

"So how did you guys meet?"

You're stumped.

"Well, actually we kind of knew each other from uni," Jamie starts saying.

You close your eyes, not wanting to watch the disaster unfolding as two of your five friends were at uni with you.

"Uni? I don't remember you there," Rosemary says.

"Well, you wouldn't exactly. I used to see Ella around the library, but I never got the chance to talk to her."

Your eyes pop open.

Jamie smiles across the table at you. "I would see her all the time studying but I didn't work up the guts to go over and speak to her. And then things happened, and I got busy and eventually I graduated. And then a few weeks ago, I randomly bumped into her again and it was like fate or whatever."

"Wow, that's amazing!"

"Fate indeed!"

After lunch everyone gathers around the tree for presents.

When it comes to your turn, you pick up one which turns out to be from Jamie. Ripping through the paper you see an old copy of A Christmas Carol by Charles Dickens with a bookmark of Caspar the ghost sticking out of it.

"Ooh! Caspar is a good bookmark for A Christmas Carol!"

You beam up at Jamie. "Thank you. It's perfect."

*****

After all your friends have left, you're in your study when you see a note on the desk:

Charlie says hello! And he thought this would be appropriate: "Men's courses will foreshadow certain ends, to which, if persevered in, they must lead," said Scrooge. "But if the courses be departed from, the ends will change."

Have a nice life and I hope it's a very long time before I see you again.

A

Author's note

This is a continuation of my story "Halloween Surprise" from the Windsor Writers Group's first anthology Windsor Tales published in 2017

15
Mother Christmas
By Adrian McBreen

Krysten Rodriguez is a woman who gets what she wants. That's why all the fuss last Christmas surprises her so much. Who knew her latest community-based triumph would go down like a pork chop at a kosher wedding? She uses her immense social skills for the betterment of society and all she gets is a kick
in the teeth.

*****

They're finishing their skinny lattes and bundling up the babies when Isabella shimmies over to take a closer look at the neighbourhood notice board. "Oh, look at this, how fun!" She claps her hands and squeals like a toddler who's had one too many Smarties. There's going to be a new Santa's grotto in that sad empty shop beside NikNaks. "We have to check it out." They wheel their phalanx of buggies around the concourse to examine the prospective location.

There's a 'Coming Soon' banner over images of reindeer surrounded by silver bells across the front door with designs of mistletoe, holly and berries draped behind the curving windows. A cartoon elf on snowy ground holds a loudspeaker that proclaims: 'Santa Claus is coming to town!' in a speech bubble. "Huh, I was almost sure another one of those wanky London franchises would open in here," says Stephanie, peering through the glass. "I'm sure there's one on the way soon enough, these plots are never empty for long."

It says there'll be an open morning to cast roles, Santa, Mrs Claus, and a collection of elves, for the grotto. Krysten snaps a photo on her phone as they're leaving and decides there and then she'll be the next Santa. She begins to make a mental note of the things she needs for her interview outfit.

Saturday morning comes round and a queue of potential Santa Clauses snakes through the market. Krysten is tall and curvy; sure, there are an extra few pounds after two kids, but a strict regimen of Pilates, hot yoga and spinning keeps the flab at bay. Her hair is a fervent golden mop, a special bronze hue that some would call dirty blonde. The ruffled aspect is somewhat lessened by her height, which bestows a certain statuesque seriousness.

Krysten buzzes in at the intercom and pats her cheeks with one final blush of paprika before going upstairs to the offices. She's always been a hurricane of entitlement, the residue of privilege; she's all swirl and noise and destruction, with nothing at the centre. She lives in a world where things must always go her way; it's a law as certain as that of gravity.

*****

It's late August and Sophia Ellison is dotting the i's and crossing the t's on her Christmas business plan in the management offices of Windsor Royal Station. They need to fill that eyesore of a space before the new tenants set up shop. She has the makings of an idea. Top of her list is final recruitment for an exciting venture this holiday season. The plan will be a crucial element in their whole Christmas Experience; yes, their season of goodwill is going to have a unique spin this year.

She barrels into the boardroom, where she's called a meeting. "As we all know, one of those reassuringly expensive shops in 'I Saw You Coming' alley has become vacant, and we can't have that. It'll be the perfect spot for a Santa's grotto with an inclusive twist." She raises her hands into air quotes. "This little 'shopping centre' is so much more than any other bland capitalist monument to corporate greed, we have history. Well, the corporate greed bit might still exist, but that's neither here nor there. Then there's that giant golden goose a few hundred yards away, a huge castle and royal beacon of the Establishment. The fact that the market's location next to a huge tourist magnet, whose visitor flow will never run dry, is another massive advantage. And let's call a spade a spade, simply affixing 'Royal' onto the name of any organisation in this country is an immediate boon to its social cachet."

"Windsor has always been a cut above the rest, we all know this; we're incredibly privileged." She smiles and gives a knowing wink to her underlings. "The kind of national and international clientele this grotto would get means it absolutely needs to be as distinctive as possible. Diversity is key here, along with exclusivity of course. We've really got to think outside the box on this one; our grotto must be as classy and elegant as the town it'll serve."

*****

Krysten digs out that fat suit she wore when she went as Barbara Cartland to her writers' group fancy dress party last year. Marcus and the kids help her sew a jolly outfit from a fluffy red dressing gown and a pair of his red trousers; they just need some white trim and oversize cuffs. She has her dad's old army boots, polished and looking good as new; then she adds a thick meringue beard by moulding some cotton wool balls together into a dry paste and tying an elastic band round the top. A pair of her mother's old black plastic glasses with jam jar lenses frames her face. Her black synthetic leather belt with its large square silver buckle completes the ensemble.

Turning up in a handmade costume will increase her chances of bagging this part; her creativity would mark her out from the rest. She'd dive right into that patriarchal cup of eggnog and stir those cinnamon sticks round and round until emerging victorious with the clove of glory. She's aiming for the top job; she is determined to walk away as a jolly old man.

Krysten drinks whiskey neat and smokes almost as much as the Victorian chimney pots on her house, all in an effort to caramelize her vocal cords and inject a hit of gravel. She even gorges on fruitcake, pudding, and mince pies with lashings of brandy butter like nobody's business, not strictly necessary but she always prides herself for going that extra mile. Any way she could add any extra weight gain to that baby paunch stubbornly hanging around her midriff since Amelia. Marcus tries to offer a reality check, while he laughs at some viral news video about that pompous 'Warren Peace' man down the street. He turns to look over the back of the couch. "I've heard of method acting, Krysten, but this is beyond the pale. Why are you going all Daniel Day-Lewis for this thing? You're playing Santa, not bloody Hamlet!"

Her dogged determination is a two-headed hydra. On the plus side, the cheerleader in her head is a constant companion. Her life of privilege has ironically thwarted her career ambitions. She'd bagged a hunky husband, had two adorable mixed-race children, Mateo and Amelie, a crucial element in the image she presents to the world. But if she's being honest, Marcus only married her for the connections; her background and wealth were a sure-fire way for him to advance his own career. Her own law degree was put on ice; she quickly realised that when you have money, university girls are to men what plankton is to a whale.

As soon as she walks into those offices, Krysten is captain of Team Too Much. A motley line of overweight men in late middle age with salty beards and cloudy glasses stand around chatting. "Hello, my name is Krysten Rodriguez, and I'll be auditioning for the role of Santa."

*****

This latest development is an absolute gift for Sophia and her market's holiday master plan. "Now boys, opportunity has come a-knocking in the shape of that woman out there, and she has quite a clang," she says with an arm stretched to the door, beyond which Krysten sits in comfortable assuredness. "And we don't look gift horses in mouths around here."

Sophia peers through the internal window blinds and smiles widely before snapping them shut and swivelling around. She looks at a pasty-faced subservient who is taking a tentative sip from his coffee. "I've heard that knock, have you, Simon?" She swings around on the chair's hinges to her marketing manager and points her pen at him like a laser beam. "And as for that cute DIY getup – that was a touch of class, it shows real initiative, sheer resourcefulness, true grit, and not to mention bloody-minded determination. Her enthusiasm fits into our mission like a glove." Her voice trails off, becoming a monologue as she begins to whisper nonsensically to herself. Her staff members avert their eyes and shift in their seats.

A series of light bulbs switch on in her brain and she takes a chewed pen from her mouth. "Listen: every bloody grotto in this country will have some round old man bleating on and on about presents and lists and shit. Well, who says the idea of 'Father Christmas' is written in stone? Windsor is nothing if not exclusive, am I right? We get a better class of person here, shall we say. So, we're going to make damn sure OUR grotto is equally exclusive. Windsor Royal Station is breaking the glass ceiling. We're going to have an all-inclusive winter season this year and that woman is going to be our secret weapon." If she had a kitten, she'd stroke it. Her staff's interest starts to pique.

"We do have a precedent here of sorts, last year's all-black production of the Nativity at St Luke's got the inclusivity ball rolling, that Bunne woman beat us to it then, not this time." Sophia continues, "But our addition this Xmas is going to be just as Woke, however this time it'll have bells on, if you'll excuse the pun," as she giggles at her own joke. "Parents spend six million quid bringing little Madison and Montana to visit the Big Guy every year. We need to start milking that cash cow. Now I want everyone on board with these plans, remember teamwork makes the dream work! Get her on board, tout suite."

*****

The grotto opens on the first weekend in November and is an immediate draw for the town's off-season tourists and local families. As if the town isn't enough of a heritage magnet, its powerful force now comes with a filter, which is channelling a large chunk of the visiting hordes directly from trains and buses into the new Winter Wonderland. Is it an added bonus or a threat? Krysten's gut feeling is for the former, she's always been a glass half-full kind of girl. Live and let live is her mantra.

From mid-December the pop-up attraction would ramp up a gear by opening every day until Christmas Eve to fully attract the winter crowds. 'Santa gets the Royal Treatment' is the headline on PR blurbs sent out to local rags. This message would soon go much, much further than that.

Red felt awnings swing over the brick shop-front and two sparkling white spruce trees stand behind a temporary picket fence while winter scenes of a snowy, grey forest cover each window. Right next to the entrance there's two cuddly reindeer guarding presents and staring intently with blood red eyes, which gives them something of the demonic look. Non-offensive melodies like 'Walking in the Air', 'Peace on

Earth/Little Drummer Boy', 'Do You Hear What I Hear?', 'Let It Snow' and a down-tempo version of 'Deck the Hall' plays from speakers. Gold and silver baubles, snow-tipped fir branches and crystal fairy lights hang on rails around the grotto.

Queues begin almost immediately every weekend morning. A line of mums, dads, babies, buggies, toddlers, older kids and vast international extended families forms between the toy train on its track and velvet ropes. They sample the complimentary gingerbread figures, with mulled wine and mince pies for the adults, while they wait. An elf rings two large bronze bells and sprinkles ice patterns; he clangs up and down the line welcoming visitors. "Are you all looking forward to seeing Santa?" he squeaks. "YES!" comes the choral response. "Well, we've been getting ready for a whole year and she's looking forward to greeting everybody today."

"Sorry?" One of the trendy fathers with a long grey coat and gelled hair smirks. "It sounded like you used the 'she' pronoun there."

"Yes. That's just what I said, sir."

Daddy Cool does a double-take and coughs up some coffee into his bamboo cup.

"You seem like a sophisticated kind of chap. We wouldn't want to reveal Santa's magic," says the elf. He cups his hands over the child's ears and whispers, "Especially not in front of the kiddies."

"Duly noted."

Sophia takes a walk around on opening weekend to see what a whopping success she's made of an empty space, is it too much to think she's now godlike? Making a creation from thin air and all. Probably stretching it a little.

One of her minions is in tow, a plump middle-manager wearing an ill-fitting suit with wide eyes and a gormless face. They pass rows of children, some bemused, some excited, some eager, while others are frankly terrified, screaming at the top of their lungs and literally shaking.

"This is going to be a great little earner, why didn't we do this sooner? We're going to be jingling all the way to the bank at this rate," she says.

"It's only meant to be a temporary attraction, boss."

"Bah humbug! Temporary shmempory, this must be an annual event; mark my words, a new holiday tradition for Windsor has just been birthed. And remember this, Bambi: I've been doing shit like this since you were an itch in your daddy's pants. Just look at all these entitled yuppies, they're lapping it up."

Local press learns of this new seasonal enticement through official releases, and they obligingly write up fawning reports. Some of the choice articles read: 'A class above your average grotto', 'By royal appointment' and 'On Her Majesty's Christmas service'. However, once they get wind of an oestrogen-fuelled protagonist at its heart, it's as if a juicy steak has just been thrown into a pack of wild animals. The story rapidly hits the Nationals, helped in no small measure by an obsequious Windsor angle. Once word lands on social media, their small magical wonderland goes viral.

Kevin shows Sophia the one thousand four hundred and twenty seventh parenting forum that first week. A thread is devoted to this 'intimate family-friendly holiday kingdom' with its 'ground-breaking diversity', and, holy of holies, 'royal connections'. They're the nice reviews; the naughty ones soon follow, and the list grows. He can't tell if she is pleased or peeved.

"What we've lost in exclusivity we've gained in notoriety it seems."

"Boss, it looks like the shit's beginning to hit the fan on this one. People are moaning about a woman taking over a traditionally male role, think about the children etcetera."

*****

Her local celebrity status appeals to Krysten at first, it wears off sooner than you can say 'magical sleigh ride' though. She simply can't understand why it's a big deal that a woman should have the audacity to play Santa Claus. Why this entire hullabaloo? Aren't we supposed to be in fourth wave feminism? Whatever happened to MeToo?

The whole shitstorm gets her thinking though. Why not go back and get that degree? After all, Krysten Rodriguez is a woman who always gets what she wants at the end of the day.

Printed in Great Britain
by Amazon

12908788R00119